Xavier

Hathaway House, Book 24

Dale Mayer

XAVIER: HATHAWAY HOUSE, BOOK 24
Beverly Dale Mayer
Valley Publishing Ltd.

ISBN-13: 978-1-778860-20-1
Print Edition

Books in This Series:

Yvonne, Book 25

Boxed Sets and Bundles
https://geni.us/Bundlepage

About This Book

Welcome to Hathaway House. Rehab Center. Safe Haven. Second chance at life and love.

Self-sabotage isn't a concept Xavier is familiar with, until he ends up at Hathaway House—his application sent in with his buddy's. When Xavier's application was accepted, but his friend's wasn't, Xavier struggles with success. Even his arrival at Hathaway is bittersweet, knowing his friend has been rushed back to the hospital.

Talia, a patient coordinator at Hathaway House, witnesses Xavier's arrival, her heart tugging at his obvious sense of guilt. Even with Xavier's stomach barely holding down food and with his mind and soul emotionally struggling without his buddy, she knows Xavier's got what it takes to make a great recovery here—if he just focuses on his own life.

Hathaway is about progress, as Xavier's about to find out, … with friends and without.

Sign up to be notified of all Dale's releases here!
https://geni.us/DaleNews

T HE ROOM WAS hot and airless with the windows closed, but, when you didn't have a private room and somebody else couldn't breathe in the cold air, you kept the window closed because it was the thing to do. But for his roommate's sake, Xavier would be outside, with that window open at all times. But it wasn't to be. He stared over at the man he had served with through many missions, not liking what he saw of his color. "Hey, do you want me to get you some help?"

Zander shook his head. "Nothing they can do, man." He turned to look at him and said, "I'm sure I got this virus here."

Xavier shrugged. "It would be hard not to, when it's going around."

"Yeah, before you get it, you should get outta here."

"I got no place to go," Xavier muttered.

"Get outta here, just get outta here. Find another center, find someplace where you could have the window open."

"You noticed that, *huh*?"

"Yeah, man. I'm sorry, but that cold air kills my lungs every time I inhale."

Xavier nodded. "That's why it's closed."

"And I appreciate it, yet you need to find another place to stay."

"Yeah? Is there even another place?"

"A friend of mine went to Hathaway House," he shared, "and he swears by it."

"I've heard that a couple times too," Xavier noted, "but the whole process to get outta here sounds painful."

"I don't think it has to be," he said, and then he started to cough again.

Xavier winced. "Man, are you sure you don't want me to call somebody?"

"Nobody to call for this," he said. "It's why I'm telling you to get outta here."

"Yeah, but it's not as if what happened to you can't happen elsewhere."

"Right, but you know something? Sometimes it's things like this that make you decide to change."

"Sure, but you're the one who's sick, so maybe *you* should be getting out of here."

"I gotta get rid of this virus first. Don't wanna be spreading it around. If I could get clearance, I would," he said.

Xavier looked at Zander, frowning. "You don't have to give up though."

"I'm not giving up," he stated, "although, man, I've come to that point a couple times."

"That's one of the reasons why I'm still kinda here."

"Don't do that. You can't throw your life away, waiting on me," he replied. "Honest to God, apply for Hathaway and get out of here."

"I'll apply if you do," Xavier murmured.

Coughing and laughing at that, Zander replied, "They already turned me down."

He stared at his friend. "Why?"

"Too soon after surgery, too many adaptations still, they

didn't have a bed, *blah, blah, blah*. They put me on a waitlist," he added, "but that's just a nice way of saying, *Sorry, no.*"

"Well, if they're like that," Xavier noted, "then I don't want to go."

Then Zander looked at him and shook his head. "Don't do that. Don't cut off your nose to spite your face," he pointed out. "You need this, and they can help you. If I had a chance of going, I would, and I would make the best I could out of it. … Besides, if you go, you can always put in a good word for me."

Xavier frowned at his friend. "I don't want to leave you here," he stated bluntly.

"You'll have to because staying here is not doing you any good."

Xavier argued, "We've been to battle together too many times for me to walk away now."

"Then step forward," Zander ordered. "Step forward and take one for the team."

He snorted at that. "You mean, take something good for the team? Yeah, that's not the way I operate."

"At this point in time I think you need to. And, if there is any chance of my getting there, then it won't hurt to at least have a reference from somebody who is there."

"Doesn't mean that they'll even accept me," Xavier stated. "Besides, if they turned you down, they would leave me hanging."

"And turning me down does not mean that they'll turn you down." Zander glared at him. "You need to try."

And, with that, Xavier gave in, somewhat less than gracefully.

Giving it a try was a whole different story than giving in.

But he expected to receive an absolute and complete no. When he got an acceptance, although it wouldn't take effect for another couple months, he was stunned. He hated to even tell Zander. Yet Zander was thrilled.

"Good, and I'm starting to feel much better too. The last dose of antibiotics helped."

"Well, getting your lung punctured and catching pneumonia at the same time, being on a ventilator too …"

"But I am slowly recovering, and that's what's given me hope," Zander declared.

"I still think I should stay though."

"No," he snapped. "You need to go." He glared at his friend. "Sometimes you have to walk alone."

"Walking alone isn't a problem," Xavier snapped, "but I don't like walking away from anybody."

"I'm not asking you to walk away," Zander murmured. "I'm asking you to go there first, to do your reconnaissance, and to report back."

At that, Xavier burst out laughing. "Okay, I can do that, but only if you promise that you will contact them every week, saying you're still looking to come. And, I mean, every week from now on, until I tell you to stop or until you hear from them that you're accepted."

"Do you think it will make any difference?" he asked doubtfully. "Won't that just piss them off?"

"Then piss them off," Xavier said. "At least it shows that you care and that you'll do everything it takes to get there. And I'll push from my side too."

"Yeah, don't you do anything to jeopardize your healing," he warned.

"I won't, but no way will I do well and not give you the exact same opportunity," Xavier declared. "Remember that."

Zander looked at him and smiled. "I'll remember it, but—just as much as I'll email them every week—I will email you and give you a virtual kick in the butt to ensure you do the best you can while there."

"While I'm there, you know it. But I'll be pissed if you can't come and join me."

"Don't hold it against them," Zander warned. "They must have rules, regulations, and limited places for people."

"Good, depending on how long it takes, we'll ensure a spot for you, so you sit tight. You're coming, whether you like it or not."

"You know I want to go," Zander said. Then he started another horrific set of coughing. But at least it seemed productive, moving around some of the congestion. And when he stared back over at Xavier, Zander smiled and said, "I really am feeling better."

"Yeah, *sure*," Xavier said in disgust.

"You need to get out of here before you catch something that'll kill you."

"Same for you," he muttered. "Same for you."

And, with that, he settled down to rest, wondering what the odds were of getting Zander into the Hathaway place while Xavier was still there. Probably not all that great odds, but he would do whatever he could. Zander had saved his life. If Xavier could return the favor now, he was up for it. In fact, he was bound and determined to do it, whether his friend liked it or not.

Chapter 1

X AVIER HORTENSE STARED around his room. It wasn't even *his* room. It was a temporary room. Apparently one of the beds that was supposed to be empty and ready for him *wasn't*. He looked back at the woman who was busy trying to give him an explanation. He just held up a hand. "It's fine. I gather you guys are busy."

"An ambulance didn't arrive to transfer our patient, which is to be your room," she added, with a nod. "So this is your room for the moment. I'll get you into your assigned room as soon as I can." She gave him a gentle smile. "Sorry. This isn't the way we normally operate."

He shrugged. "I've waited a long time, so I guess it doesn't really matter."

"It matters," she stated. "And it's still not the way we normally do business. So, as soon as I can, we'll get you into your own space." And, with that, she disappeared.

But he didn't get a chance to do much of anything before another woman walked in, a notepad in her hand, looking up, smiling at him. "Hey. I understand you just got here, and we don't have a room for you."

He smiled at her. "That's what I understand. Glad it's not a big deal."

"No, and it doesn't happen often," she shared, "but we have hundreds of people here at any given time, so, when things like an ambulance doesn't show up or Patient Care doesn't show up or whatever the case maybe, it can have a domino effect."

He nodded. "And who are you?"

"Oh, sorry." She flashed him a smile. "Talia Sweetling. I arrange some of the programs here. I'm a coordinator."

He nodded. "So you're trying to coordinate me a room?"

"Nope, Dani's off doing that right now."

"Dani?"

She nodded toward the door. "The woman who just left."

"Ah." Xavier nodded. "She did tell me that she would get me into my room soon."

"Oh, you have one slotted. It just didn't get emptied," Talia stated, with a sigh. "We're working on it."

He nodded. "And what do you coordinate?"

"All kinds of programs, including yoga, day trips, horse-back riding, *blah, blah, blah.*" She grinned good-naturedly at him. "If you want to do anything, and we don't offer it, just let me know. I'll see if I can find somebody to teach it."

He stared at her. "Did you say yoga?"

"I did, indeed."

"Wow, I don't think I'll be anywhere close to doing yoga for a very long time."

"You never know," she said, studying him. "I teach yoga. So, if you want to take a class, I would be happy to have you there."

"I don't think so," he replied, with a headshake. "I want to sleep through the night and get through the day like a normal person, not with my legs going out from under me or my back giving way and crumpling me to the ground."

"Ah." She nodded. "So, in other words, health first."

"Exactly," he agreed. "And now you're supposed to tell me that they aren't mutually exclusive."

"They sure aren't," she confirmed, with a big grin. "Yet you aren't the first one to think that. Priorities in your world basically come down to health and fitness before yoga."

"I guess not too many people want to do yoga, *huh?*"

"Lots of them do," she clarified, with a bright smile. "The ones who don't are the ones who have never done it before and don't understand its benefits."

He stared at her. "So yoga has benefits?" She burst out into peals of laughter that found an answering tug on his lips. "Well, you've given me something to smile about today, which I wasn't so sure would happen."

Immediately she frowned at him. "What's the matter?"

"You mean, outside of the fact that life sucks?"

"Yeah, outside of that."

"In the VA Center I just left, I had to leave behind my best buddy. We went through two tours in Iraq together," he began. "I wasn't even sure about coming here without him, but he wanted me to come ahead anyway. Then he got really sick just before I left. I still don't even know if he's survived."

She stared at him. "I am so sorry, and, of course, it's worse now that you're here because you feel cut off."

He nodded. "I do."

"What's his name?" she asked, clicking her pen.

"Why? You'll phone the VA Center and see if he's okay?"

"I presume you've already tried to call him directly?"

He nodded. "No answer."

"So then, yes, I'll phone the VA Center and see if we can get an update." When he frowned, she shrugged. "That's just the right thing to do, so you can expect us to go the extra mile here."

"I'm surprised, but, yes, please call. His name is Zander Tolston."

"It'll take me a little bit to get through," she began, "so do you want a cup of coffee or anything while we wait for your room to be ready?"

He shrugged. "I don't know that I could keep anything down right now."

"Fine. Let me get you some updated information on Zander, and then we'll go from there." And, with that, she darted off.

TALIA RACED TO her office, ignoring all the chaos going on around her. Some days were like this. Most were not. But they had enough problems and logistical issues that only so much could be done, and it would take a little time to solve them. However, confirming Zander's status was something she could solve right now. She made the phone call, and, when she got patched through to the admitting office, she asked them about the health status of this Zander. She quickly explained who was asking and why.

"Ah, right," replied the lady on the other end. "Xavier just left the VA today."

"Yes, that's correct, and he's arrived here at Hathaway House, but he's pretty worried about his friend Zander."

"The two of them were inseparable," the woman shared.

"*Were?*" Talia asked.

"Sorry. He's not dead. That's a turn of phrase because Zander isn't right here. Let me see what I can find out."

Talia was put on hold and stood here waiting and waiting and wondering if everybody's life was as chaotic as theirs. At that moment the woman came back on the phone.

"He's been taken to Emergency," she declared. "I don't have an update from this afternoon, but this morning Zander was breathing on his own. Yet he does appear to have a bad case of pneumonia."

"Xavier told me that Zander had pneumonia already."

"He also has compromised lungs, so any case of pneumonia is a big deal."

"Right," Talia agreed. "What hospital?" Writing down the name of the hospital, she ended the call with, "Thank you." Then she headed back down to where Xavier still sat, staring out the window.

He looked up when she walked in, took one look at her face, and replied, "It's not good news, is it?"

"It's not terribly bad news either," she clarified, "so let's keep that in mind. Your friend's been taken back to the hospital for pneumonia."

He nodded at that. "He had pneumonia before."

"Seems his lungs are compromised."

He winced at that. "I was really hoping that he could beat this. He's been trying to come here for ages but always has a health setback."

"Just because he's got pneumonia doesn't mean he can't come here. It just means he's probably not strong enough to make the trip."

"Exactly," Xavier noted, resting his head back. "I told him that I would wait with him until he was stronger, but he wanted me to come ahead."

"And that sounds like a good thing. We can't do everything for everyone, the way what hospitals can do. Yet obviously he wants you to be here to get whatever benefit you can in the meantime."

"Maybe. Did they say what hospital?"

She nodded. "I wrote it down for you, and I'll check again later today," she offered. "Now that we've got that little bit of news—and it's not enough yet, but we're working on it—can I get you a cup of coffee?"

He nodded. "That would be quite nice, thank you. I appreciate it. ... I would get it myself, but I don't know where I'm going."

She smiled at him. "Would you like to see?"

He nodded. "It's better than sitting here and doing nothing."

She handed him her notepad. "You hang on to that, and we'll head to the dining room, and see if you want something else to go with your coffee."

"I'm not very hungry," he replied.

"That can change as soon as you see the food here."

"I didn't eat much at the other place either," he shared. "Food doesn't generally appeal anymore."

"Well, let's see."

As she pushed him down the hallway, he looked around and muttered, "It's a big place."

"It *is* a big place and getting bigger all the time."

"You guys are expanding?"

"We are. We just seem to be in a constant state of growth here."

"That's a good thing."

"Yes, but the logistics of catching up on the staff requirements while we add more patients can be a struggle."

"And more beds," he noted, with a sigh.

"We're getting your bed ready, and housekeeping's in there right now. I figured we could get you a coffee first, and then I'll take you to your room, where you can relax in your own space."

"Thank you."

Chapter 2

TALIA PUSHED XAVIER forward in his wheelchair through the dining room and looked up to see Dennis watching them approach.

"Hey, seems we have somebody new."

"Yeah, this is Xavier. Xavier, this is Dennis. He runs the kitchen more or less, although Ilse is the main chef in the back."

Xavier smiled at Dennis. "Hey. Apparently coffee is around here someplace."

"There is, indeed. And food, if you would like something."

At that, Xavier shook his head. "I'm not big on food."

Dennis's eyebrows peaked instantly. "Whoa, whoa, whoa. What do you mean that you're not big on food?" he asked. "Food is mandatory nutrition for your body. If you're not getting that, we'll have to get you hooked up on my special shakes."

"Shakes are okay," Xavier replied. "I just don't have much of an appetite anymore."

Talia pushed him to the coffee area. "This is the coffee station. It's open most of the time. Usually you will find a little bit in the way of treats too."

"Yeah, treats don't really interest me either." Xavier eyed the coffee and nodded. "Black coffee, just as it is, please."

15

She quickly poured him a cup and looked over at Dennis to see the shock on his face. "You're upsetting Dennis."

Xavier looked over at the other man. "Why?"

"Because food matters to Dennis," she explained. "And to even think that you might not be big on food will give him sleepless nights."

When Dennis joined them, Xavier explained, "I just don't have an appetite, so what am I supposed to do? It's not as if I can just keep shoving food in. It comes right back up."

Dennis frowned at him. "What food do you like?"

"I used to like meat," he replied, "but it all tastes like sawdust."

"Ah." At that, the expression on Dennis's face cleared. "What about sweets?"

Xavier shrugged. "It's never been my big thing."

At that, Dennis held up one finger and entered the kitchen area behind the door and returned shortly. "These just came out of the oven. Do they appeal?" And he held out a tray of cinnamon buns.

She smiled down as Xavier eyed them. "I don't want to insult you, but I don't know. I hate to waste food, and I probably wouldn't eat it."

But Dennis wasn't taking no for an answer. He grabbed two plates and scooped one bun onto each, along with a fork apiece. "If you don't like it, that's not a really big bun anyway."

"I don't want to waste food," Xavier repeated.

"Good. I'm glad you don't want to waste food. We have a policy about that here."

"Which is why I rarely even try most foods anymore," Xavier explained, "because so often it doesn't taste right. And it all comes back up. Then I feel bad. So it's best if I just don't even bother taking it."

"Got it," Dennis said, with a smile. "For now just try it. If you can't finish it, no hard feelings."

"Okay," Xavier conceded. He looked back at Talia. "Are we taking this back to my room?"

"Unless you want to sit out on the deck for a little bit and have it out there, while they finish off your room."

He stared at the deck and beyond, nodding now. "That would be good. Is that deck available for people?"

"Absolutely it's available for people. And, yes, people like you," she added, with a smile.

Dennis walked ahead, carrying the plated cinnamon buns and took them out to the deck.

Xavier stopped when he saw all the animals in the pastures. "Good Lord." He took several slow, deep breaths. "So I'm allowed to sit on the deck?"

"You are, as long as the kitchen's open," Dennis clarified. "I do lock it up overnight, but, other than that, I'm here early, and I generally don't leave until late either."

At that, Talia laughed. "Honestly, he's always here. So if you need anything from the kitchen, he's the one to help you." She studied Xavier's features, as he stared at Dennis, wondering at the luck. She leaned over and added, "Yes, he means it. Everybody here does."

Xavier nodded slowly but hesitantly, as if not sure how to react.

She'd seen it every once in a while with new patients, but nothing quite so pronounced as this time. She asked him, "Are you okay?"

"I'm okay," he stated, shaking off whatever was bothering him. "It'll just take a bit to get used to a new system."

"It will," Dennis agreed. "Still, I think you'll adjust faster than you expect." And, with that, Dennis turned and walked away.

XAVIER TURNED TO Talia. "Did I insult him?"

"Dennis is fine, just worried about all of us," she said. "He'll watch you like a hawk to see what foods you readily eat and what others he can tempt you to eat."

"I just don't want to waste anything," he mentioned once again. "The VA really jumped on us about the waste."

"Curtailing the waste is important, but here it's not quite such a stringent deal."

"It should be though, maybe," he pointed out. "Food shouldn't be wasted, not with all the hungry people in the world."

"And I get that. Now are you more worried about the environment, about the cost, or just the fact that some food ends up as no good to anybody?"

He shrugged. "I don't have any right to be worried about anything. My plate's pretty full just thinking about trying to get through my days," he explained in a quiet tone. "But I guess it just feels wrong to think of people all over the world needing food, and here I've got so much that I take it and don't eat it. So I feel compelled to eat it, but then I don't usually enjoy it."

"Don't eat food if you don't enjoy it," she declared. "Nobody'll force you into that. And, if it comes down to you not eating enough, then that's a whole different story, but that's not my problem. That's between you and your doctors."

Xavier nodded. "It hasn't come to that. Yet all the food

tastes like sawdust to me, so then I just can't get it down. Or maybe it's because I know it'll come back up."

"Yet our food is delicious, so I don't know how any of it could possibly taste like sawdust. Believe me, these guys know how to cook."

He looked at her doubtfully.

She smiled. "You don't have to take my word for it," she muttered. "Just try the cinnamon bun."

"And if I don't like it?" he asked hesitantly, staring down at the treat. Yet, when he sniffed the air, he started to smile. "It does smell good."

"It should more than smell good," she said, as she sat beside Xavier and ripped into hers. "It tastes wonderful."

He watched as she devoured hers and asked, "Am I taking you away from work?"

She shook her head. "Nope, not right now you aren't. So don't worry about me. Just enjoy your coffee and your cinnamon bun. Everything else is secondary."

He wasn't even sure what to think about that because, in his world, everything was secondary to his health and his rehab. He had a schedule to adhere to, to focus on exactly what needed to be done at that moment. But it seemed fairly relaxed here at Hathaway. At least for right now. He took a bite of the cinnamon bun, a small one, and frowned. Then he took another bite. "It's nice and fresh," he noted.

"It is, and everybody here really enjoys their groceries, so you'll find all kinds of extra treats on a regular basis."

"Ah, and that probably is why Dennis was shocked that I don't generally eat much."

"Of course, but that's okay. If you're not happy eating the food on offer here on any given day, then tell Dennis what you want. I don't know how much individual catering he can do because the kitchen prepares a large amount of food for a large amount of people every day, three times a day. Still, we try to accommodate everyone. If he can get you something different, he'll do it because he's a nice guy, just like the rest of us."

He frowned at her, and she nodded. "We have a very different place here," she explained. "And I get that that may sound cliché, but it's really not. It won't take you long to adjust, so give yourself some time and just relax with it all."

Xavier thought about her words long after he had been shown to his assigned room and left in peace and quiet. So far he'd been impressed with the place, not so much about the location—although the glimpse he'd caught outside made him want to go to the grassy yard and just spend time sitting there with the animals. However, he had been more impressed with the people, the staff, and the apparent caring in their hearts. He figured it would wear off soon enough. He was used to more indifference than anything else from medical personnel. However, already Xavier felt as if the staff here was friendlier, not so much of a working relationship.

And there was both good and bad to that. It was good as long as everything worked, but the minute a problem surfaced, it sucked because then you didn't want to complain because they were friends. Yet, if they weren't doing their job, that made for a much tougher environment to live in.

Xavier wasn't a complainer by nature, but he'd certainly complained lots on Zander's behalf. Zander needed more. He needed his bedding changed more often, and he needed an extra hand with his shower. His body was way weaker, his muscles atrophied. Yet every time Xavier had gone to bat for Zander, his buddy got mad and said that he was fine. But he wasn't fine. He just always said that because he didn't want to cause anybody any extra trouble.

Xavier was sure that's why Zander ended up even sicker. He should have been looking after himself and should have reminded the staff to do that too. But then who was Xavier to talk? He was here, in his own room, wondering why he'd even bothered leaving his buddy, when this move should be about him and not Zander.

However, Xavier was always wondering if Zander was okay, wondering if he would get out of that hospital before he needed more drugs. Zander was a good guy, but he couldn't fight for himself. Thus, with Xavier leaving him behind, it felt as if Xavier had deserted Zander. Xavier felt like a heel all over again.

Chapter 3

THE FIRST THING Talia did the next morning when she walked into her office was phone the hospital to check up on Zander's progress. The news was encouraging, and, with that, she headed down to see Xavier. When she knocked on his door, he answered.

"Come in."

He looked up to see who it was, and she stepped inside. "Hey. I didn't know if you'd connected with the hospital regarding your friend yet, but I did just now. I have an update." She quickly filled him in on Zander's condition. "They've changed out his medication, and he seems to be doing better."

"That is good news," Xavier replied. "Zander is not good at fighting for himself."

"No, but he seems to have a wingman who will fight for him," she noted, with a bright smile.

"Yeah." Xavier nodded. "He saved my life. And I still feel as if I deserted him by leaving him back there."

"And what did he want you to do?"

"He wanted me to come ahead and to get his place ready," Xavier shared, with a chuckle.

"Then why don't you do that?" she asked. "Keep him informed of your progress and how this place is, what you would like to change, what you think he would like, and just give him a running commentary. When he gets here"—and she deliberately didn't say *if*—"he'll feel comfortable and will settle in faster."

He eyed her and then nodded. "I don't know if it works that way, but I could definitely do that for him."

"So then do it," she urged. "Obviously he needs something to look forward to right now, while he gets over this current illness."

"He's had nothing but illnesses," Xavier shared.

"And that could be the reason why we can't have him here just yet," she pointed out. "I don't know. That would be left up to the doctors back there and to our doctors here."

Xavier nodded. "That's really a concern for him too."

"And I'm sure for you as well. Has Zander shared his health issues with you?"

"His immune system's shot," Xavier said. "Seems as if he catches everything."

"I'm sorry. That takes longer to build up, especially when you have back-to-back bouts of pneumonia."

"Then after that hurdle, Zander has to get the funding for a stay here. I have no idea what it costs at a place like this."

"Dani works on getting funding for everybody she can. After all, our patients are all veterans. It does depend on if we are the right place to help our patients with rehab. Like your friend Zander is in a hospital. We can't treat patients here when they really need to be in a hospital setting. However, if rehab is on the agenda, then Dani will see about getting it funded, even partially if not fully."

Xavier frowned. "I hope that's true. Zander and I were injured out on a mission, so I don't think that it should be a problem, but ... who knows? It seems as if a problem always pops up somewhere."

"Then I wouldn't worry about it," she suggested. "Let's get you into your rehab program, while Zander gets a little bit stronger. Then, when we do get him moved here, he should adjust faster, having updates from you beforehand."

Xavier smiled at that. "I don't think anybody would call him slow."

"Maybe not, but his body might balk," she noted, with a gentle smile. "This is all about dealing with your bodies and what they need. And it's not always what we think that they need."

"No, it never is, is it?" he agreed, shrugging.

"Did you have a good night?" she asked.

"It was okay. I kept waking up and falling back under and waking up yet again. I was worried about Zander's healing, my acclimating to my strange bed, and, to a different scenario, enduring all the traveling. Everything was just going over and over in my mind."

"That's pretty normal for new patients to go through," she confirmed. "Your medical team can offer you some sleep aids, from prescriptions to more homeopathic remedies. The new guys get a day or two off to settle in. Then you get tested to see where they should start you off. Your rehab program will be tailored for your starting point, and then you start seeing some of your medical team. So ask any of them about any problems sleeping or whatever."

He nodded. "Maybe."

She got the distinct feeling that that was a flat-out no. Yeah, most of these veterans refused to ask for help. She asked him, "Did you get down for breakfast?"

He shook his head. "Am I supposed to get down there on my own?" he asked. "I wasn't sure what the protocol was."

"It depends on how mobile you are after your travels and if you're too tired."

"I'm not too tired." He sat up in bed.

She noted that he was fully dressed. "Then let's go. I want some coffee anyway."

He frowned. "You're not on babysitting duty again, are you?"

She laughed. "No, no babysitting duty in my world," she replied. "First thing I did was make a phone call to check on your friend's progress and after that? I have plenty to keep me busy for the rest of the day."

He nodded. "If you wouldn't mind, I would appreciate your taking me to the dining room again. Otherwise I can go down there on my own."

Still turning down help, even when offered. Talia smiled. "Nope, I'll take you down. Maybe, if we're lucky, we'll find more cinnamon buns."

"Do they keep them around all the time?" he asked curiously.

"No. You have to be lucky enough to be there in time to get them."

"Ah. I consider myself much more of a meat-eater, so, if I miss them, I'll be okay with that."

"Well, how did the cinnamon bun go down yesterday?"

He nodded. "Fine. It was really fresh tasting."

"That's because it was made fresh, right before they came out of the oven. So that's really not a surprise."

"Maybe for you," he said, "but for me? It's a surprise."

"Well, come on then. Let's go see what other surprises they have for us today," she stated, with a bright smile. She waited for him to get into his wheelchair and went to push him, but he raised a hand.

"I'll do it."

"If you're sure?" she asked. "You just got here, and we don't want to tire you further than your travels already did. We can't have you suffer a setback for trying too hard."

He frowned over at her.

"That's why we give every new arrival a couple days to get in sync with being here. If you get tired or too exhausted at the get-go, there really is no benefit in it for anybody." His shoulders slumped, and she added, "And didn't you say that sometimes your back gives out on you and your knees, et cetera?"

"Yeah, sure. Doesn't that happen to everybody?"

"Not sure it does," she said, "but I'm not one of the medical professionals here, so I have no clue."

TALIA'S ANSWER WAS honest and forthright, followed by a gurgle of laughter, which brought a smile to Xavier's face. "Are you always this upbeat and happy?" he asked.

"Yep, pretty much. Does it bother you?"

"No, it's quite nice. After getting used to people not wanting to do their jobs or not being in a job that they enjoy, it ruins the day for the rest of us."

"Or the week or the month or the lifetime," she added in agreement.

He burst out laughing. "I wasn't thinking it was quite that bad," he muttered, with a smile.

"Good. I'm glad to hear that."

He looked up at her, as she pushed him down the hall-way. "I guess I'm just surprised that you're upbeat and happy all the time that I've known you."

"Which is a whole *what*? Half a day?"

He laughed. "That's true. … I guess you have time yet."

"Time for what?" she asked curiously.

Without cracking a grin, he replied, "To see your grumpy side."

She dropped down so that he could see a big frown on her face. "*This* is my grumpy side," she stated.

He started to chuckle.

"No, look. This is it. … This is me being grumpy."

He snorted. "That's you being a clown."

Immediately her face cracked up again. "Now that could be true, but the truth of the matter is, I don't get upset very easily. And, in a place like this, that's a godsend. Because upsets and emotions and tempers and frustrations can all run high at times. How can it not? People are in the middle of a transition here at Hathaway House."

"Is that what you guys call it here, a *transition*?" he asked.

"Yes."

"Transition to what?" he asked, twisting to look up at her.

"Transition to the best life that you get to live," she replied. "Each of our patients has come from somewhere," she declared, throwing out an arm with an expansive gesture.

Xavier saw dozens of people in the buffet line and even dozens more in the dining room.

"But they're all in transition to what comes next," she declared. "And you may not know it now, but you're blessed to be here."

Chapter 4

TALIA WALKED INTO the office the next morning and stretched.

"Hey, looks as if you're ready to take one of your own yoga classes," Dani teased, coming up behind her.

"I should be, but I don't have any scheduled right now."

"Anytime you want to take some of that exercise space and use it for a stretch or a few minutes of yoga, go for it," Dani offered, looking over at her. "If nobody's in the yoga room, it's welcome to be used."

"And yet I always figure that, if I were there," she shared, "it would stop other people from thinking they could use it."

Dani frowned, then shrugged. "I hadn't thought of it in that way. My first impression was that everybody would pile in, thinking they had missed out on a notification of a yoga class."

Talia laughed. "That's possible too. I just don't want to stop any patient from doing what they need to be doing. "Besides, this office is big enough for a few stretches."

"When is your first class?"

"Later this morning, just before lunch."

"Good, let me know how it goes."

"Then you let me know how the patients take to having yoga available," she replied. "I'm more than willing to run the classes, but I don't want to waste everybody's time if nobody wants yoga."

"Oh, I haven't heard any complaints yet," Dani said, giving her a smile. "So I wouldn't worry about that."

Talia laughed. "Says you, but plenty of people have other things to do here, so I don't want it to become an issue."

"That'll be something we'll look at in a few weeks," Dani noted. "If we don't have any attendance, then we could reconsider it."

"Right," Talia agreed. "Anyway I've got work to do before then."

She sat down at her desk and started her workday. She had quite a bit to do, and it never got any easier nor less voluminous. And that always blew her away because you would think that there would be an end date for some of these projects, as each one finished. Yet invariably another ten dozen popped in. It was really quite irritating at times. When her timer went off on her phone, she realized she had ten minutes to start her class.

She set those reminders on purpose, so she would get a warning to get down there and to de-stress herself a few minutes before everybody showed up. She headed to the large designated room, an overflow therapy room, and opened up the windows, opened up the door, and set up some really peaceful, calm music. A lot of yoga teachers put on something really high energy, but, for everybody here, she just wanted them to calm down and to find a way to decompress.

As soon as that was set up, she rolled out her mat and sat in the center of it in the front of the room and just worked on her deep breathing. Xavier popped into her mind. He was an interesting character. She had to wonder how he was getting on. She knew he was a survivor, but she wasn't at all sure that he was a thriver. She almost chuckled at that coining of the word. Because to her it meant something, but that didn't mean it meant anything to anybody else.

She didn't get a chance to worry about it further because people started showing up for class. She watched as several of the patients came in, a couple on a pair of the usual crutches, a couple on arm crutches or whatever they were called. Those attached to the lower arm and helped stabilize them as they walked forward. A couple came in on wheelchairs. One guy looked really tired. "Hey, Steve. How're you doing?"

"Too tired to walk, I can tell you that," he muttered. "I almost didn't come."

"Well, I appreciate that you did," Talia replied. "The workout will make you feel better by the time you're done."

"And that," Steve said, "is why I'm here. Every other time I've felt better afterward. It's just hard to force myself to come when I'm so exhausted."

She nodded. "Any chance you're doing too much in rehab?"

He cracked a smile. "That's probably exactly what it is, but you just want to do what you can do."

"Oh, I get it," she murmured.

She waited a few more minutes for more people to straggle in and then shared, "We'll give everybody else a couple more minutes to come in and join us. Meanwhile, everybody sit on your mats. And, if anybody needs a hand, let me know."

She hopped up and walked around, but everybody, although slower than maybe they would have liked, managed to get onto their mat themselves. As soon as she realized that everybody was here who was coming, she looked up the hallway and then closed the door. "Okay, now let's begin."

What should have been a forty-minute session took an hour today. Yet she needed to spend that extra time with these people attending her class.

By the time her session was done, she looked at everybody and asked, "How do you feel?"

Steve muttered, "As if I could go home and sleep."

"Maybe that's what you should do," she murmured.

He nodded. "It is almost lunchtime though," he noted, "so maybe food first and then a nap."

"And by then, you probably won't want a nap."

"You could be right. Something about yoga is very invigorating in a way. It's just it doesn't hold."

"It holds until something jars you off course," she noted. "So the more you do yoga, the more you can stay on course and the less jarring every incident in life becomes."

He stared at her. "If that's true, I would spend more time trying to make that happen."

"It is true. While you're here, you have a lot of things that jar you off course. Yet, once you get back to whatever *normal* in life is for you," she explained, "that should ease back too. In fact, it should ease back even here because you're gaining so much on a daily basis."

"I am," he murmured. "Yet it feels sometimes as if I'm also losing."

"Maybe you're expending additional energy to work a different set of muscles." She watched Steve as he got up and back into his wheelchair and slowly made his way to his room.

One of the other women, Rose, looked at her and smiled. "He's always a negative person anyway."

"Maybe," she murmured. "It's hard to see somebody who's always so tired."

Rose nodded. "We all are, since the rehab sessions here are pretty intense. We work hard. We eat right, and yet it still seems as if sometimes it's never enough."

After that depressing comment, Talia wasn't at all sure about making conversation with anybody else. She made her way back to her office and sat down.

Dani popped in and asked, "How'd it go?"

"I thought it went fine, but everybody seems really tired."

"But then it's lunchtime, right?"

Talia nodded.

"So most of them have just come out of psych therapy or they've come out of physiotherapy," Dani pointed out. "Both sessions are guaranteed to exhaust you, emotionally and physically."

"Right, I wonder if we would be better off doing yoga at a different time of day," Talia wondered.

"Maybe. Ask them about that. The other alternative is to do it first thing in the morning, but not everybody wants to get up even earlier."

"And not only that," Talia said, "everybody takes a little bit longer to first get up, to get moving each day."

"Exactly," Dani agreed, with a smile. "So I would probably keep the yoga where it is for the moment, but poll your people who attend and see what they have to say."

"Good idea."

"By the way," Dani added, as she stopped and looked back at her, "how many did you have?"

"Seventeen," she shared.

Dani's mouth formed a circle. "Wow. I would have been happy if you had had four."

"We've had more than ten every day that I've offered a

class," she stated.

"That is very good news," Dani said. "I'll have to consider that."

"Consider what?"

"Just wondering how we can work it into a full-time basis, maybe for everybody to attend."

"I don't know. I think it should be left as an option," Talia recommended.

Dani stared at her. "In what way?"

"If it becomes something they *have* to do, then it becomes a chore, then it stresses them out and adds more to their need to decompress."

Dani burst out laughing. "Very good point. I'll think about it." And, with that, she dashed off.

Tired herself, and yet feeling much calmer and more peaceful after her yoga session, Talia got up, walked out of her office, and headed down for lunch. In theory, with a nice big salad under her belt, that should perk her up. As she walked in, she found all kinds of salads. "What is this today?" she asked. "Salad celebration day?"

"Hey, Ilse has tried a few new recipes." Dennis gave her a big smile. "You like salads, right?"

"I love salads," Talia declared. "What have we got to try today?" And before she knew it, she had five different salads on her plate. "Wow. I'll be lucky if I can eat all of these, but I definitely want to taste every one of them. I came down here expecting to have a nice green salad for my lunch."

"And you got it," Dennis stated, "and so much more."

She snorted. "I did at that. I did at that." She took her plate outside in the sunshine, but, as soon as she sat here, it was already too hot. The heat alone would sap the rest of her strength. As she got up to change tables, she watched as

Xavier tried awkwardly to make his way to a table, monitoring the tray in his lap, while he powered his wheelchair. She stepped up and asked, "Do you want a hand?"

"Is it wrong if I say yes?" he asked, not looking up.

"No, not at all. You'll get steadier the longer you are here."

"Says you," he muttered. "It hasn't happened yet."

"You haven't been here long enough to make anything happen," she said. She took the tray from him and suggested, "How about you get yourself up to a table."

"I can do that." He looked around and asked, "But which table?"

"Pick one, any one, although I can already tell you that it is too hot on the deck for me to eat outside."

He slid her a look. "Would you mind taking pity on me and sitting with me, so I don't have to eat alone?"

"You got it. And it's hardly taking pity on you," she noted in a droll tone. "Everybody here would be more than happy to share the table with you."

He shrugged. "I don't know anybody else."

"Ah, missing Zander, are you?"

"Always," he said.

She nodded and pointed. "Let's sit over here."

"Where's your plate?" he asked.

"It's outside. I was just looking for another place to sit that wouldn't be quite so hot."

"The heat at this hour shouldn't be so hot," he muttered. "So it'll be a scorcher of a day, won't it?"

"It sure will. So let's stay inside with the AC."

He looked at her and then nodded with approval. "I wouldn't argue that. I do find that I get much more tired when I'm overheated."

"I think everybody does," she murmured. She brought her plate over and sat down beside him. As several other people joined them at their table, Talia whispered, "There you go." She quickly made introductions and then proceeded to eat her salads. When she got to the potato salad, she cried out.

Xavier frowned at her and asked, "What's the matter?"

"It's hot. Ilse's trying out a bunch of salads, but I wasn't expecting a hot one."

At that, Dennis appeared at her side. "It's a hot German salad."

She nodded. "That vinaigrette gives it quite a bite."

"Too much of a bite?" he asked.

"No, I really like that." She took another bite and savored it for a moment. "Wow, that's really good."

"Well, keep trying the others. Ilse's hoping for a full report."

Talia laughed. "Am I supposed to send her an e-mail afterward?"

"Yes, that would be great if you would," Dennis replied. She looked at him to see if he was serious, and he shrugged. "How else do we get feedback about some of the dishes that we try?"

"Agreed, now leave me alone, and I'll sit here and eat and figure it out."

And, with that, he disappeared again.

Xavier looked over at her. "You have a really relaxed attitude to the other staff here."

"We're all good friends," she replied. "Dennis knows perfectly well that I would never say anything mean or bad to anybody here. So, when I'm telling him to get lost, he knows how it's intended."

Xavier nodded. "I don't have that relationship with anybody here. I would be afraid of overstepping my big feet."

She laughed. "I wouldn't worry about it. Very few people take offense over slights like that, … and they're not intended to be taken that way. Plus, we all have our work schedules to meet, so there is that consideration too."

"Good to know." He looked around. "Is it you that brought all the people to the table?" he asked in a low voice.

"Most people here have lives that you already understand," she pointed out. "They're missing friends, family, and so, from their point of view, lunch with anybody is often better than lunch with nobody."

He stared at her. "Meaning that a lot of people would have been happy to sit here with me because they too want company?"

"That's a good way to look at it, yes." She smiled at him. "Does that make sense?"

"Yep, it does." He put down his fork and sat back.

"What's the matter?" Talia asked.

"Nothing. I'm just … I think I'm done."

She looked down at his plateful of food and said, "You haven't hardly eaten anything."

"I know, but my stomach's not feeling really good."

"Something else to talk to the doctor about," she said. "I know all kinds of stuff that you can get to help settle your stomach. You could be reacting to one of your medicines as well. The doc can figure it out."

"Maybe. I haven't got that far with any of my appointments yet. Nothing that the other center gave me helped at all."

"Ah." She nodded. "I guess that is a concern, but everybody has a different way of looking at things."

"Somebody even suggested acupuncture."

"Hey, why not?" she replied. "Don't knock it until you try it."

"Have you ever had it done?"

She shook her head. "No, but to get something to work where traditional medicine didn't seem to work, I would be the first one to sign up for anything nontraditional." He stared at her, and she laughed. "First, talk to the doctors here, even to Shane. They all care, and, if they have any solutions for your tummy, then they'll be more than happy to help you out. Because when Dennis sees that you haven't eaten," she murmured, "he'll worry, and he'll break out the green smoothies."

He frowned at her. "Are they good?"

"Depends on what he thinks you need the most of. You might want to make your exit before Dennis sees your plate." Xavier stared at her, as she laughed. "Don't worry about it. Everybody has some upset tummy issues when they first arrive. You aren't alone. Some people here don't have all of their stomachs left."

He nodded. "Mine took a hit, but I've still got it. I did lose some of the small intestine, but I still got the bulk of it."

"So you have the basic parts, just need some tweaking to make it work."

"Tweaking?"

She shrugged. "Okay, that didn't make much sense, but the guys here can help you."

"Maybe, it just feels odd."

"What, to ask somebody here about that? I wouldn't take it that way, if I were you. People here just want to help."

"Maybe. I'll have to see."

Just then her phone alarm went off. "Have to go," she

said, standing up, reaching for her dishes.

"Do you always respond to that thing?"

"Yeah, it's the only way I keep organized," she muttered. "I have a lot of work to be done, so it keeps me hopping."

He nodded. "And that hopping would drive me crazy. Plus, I hate alarms of any kind."

She smiled. "The thing is, you have to find what works for you. So give yourself a chance to try whatever is offered and know that whatever they do here will come from the heart to improve your life. Is it a guarantee it'll help? Nope, sure isn't. But you can't go wrong if you at least try."

And, with that, she picked up her plate, dropped it off in a nearby dish bin, and dashed back to her office.

XAVIER WATCHED TALIA disappear to return to work. With Dennis now arriving, Xavier winced and slowly pushed away from the table. But he was too slow.

Dennis frowned at him. "Can't get any more down?"

Xavier shook his head. "I'm really sorry, but my stomach is just not doing very well."

"We'll get that fixed up right away," Dennis stated. "How about a green shake, heavy on the nutrients?"

"Are they terrible?" Xavier asked cautiously. "If they are, my stomach won't handle it well either, and it will come right back up."

"How about we start off with something full of enzymes and good healthy bugs in it?" he suggested. "We'll see if we can get you to start digesting some of the food that you need."

"Is that what's the problem?" he teased. "The food goes

in, but it just doesn't go through."

"Yeah, we can work on that," Dennis murmured. "Sit tight, and I'll get you a shake. The food you ate today wasn't enough to keep anybody alive. And definitely not enough to do any testing or a rehab workout. You're new here, but Shane will understand."

Xavier wasn't so sure about that, but he didn't know how to get away without appearing to be rude. And, of all the things that he'd been told in his life, he was not to be rude. As he sat here, waiting, he wondered if he would miss some appointments.

When Dennis came back with a bright green drink, Xavier eyed it. "Well, it's bright enough," he murmured. "I just don't know if it's very drinkable." Cautiously he took a small sip and then another one. He looked over at Dennis. "Actually that tastes really good."

"Glad to hear it," Dennis replied, "and you don't have to guzzle it. Take it with you. If you'll see Shane today, even better. Tell him about your stomach. And sip the green drink throughout the afternoon, so everything will have time to go down slowly. That way maybe your stomach won't revolt."

"Got it," Xavier replied. "I am a little nervous too, so that's probably part of my stomach upset."

"Nerves can do that," Dennis agreed. "Don't you worry about it. We'll get you fixed up."

And honestly, Xavier wondered if everybody was invested in his stomach because, over the next several days, the chef came out from behind the door, introduced herself, and asked if he knew of some foods that his stomach could handle. If so, she would prepare those foods for him. He'd been flustered and astonished that anybody would even care, would go to the trouble of cooking meals just for him. After talking with Ilse for about fifteen minutes, she'd already devised a menu that would be a little easier on him.

He frowned, feeling a bit embarrassed even. "I'm not trying to be difficult. I don't need anything special."

"It's not special," Ilse clarified. "You're a patient, and you get the same care as everybody else." And, with that, she bustled off again.

Xavier frowned over at Dennis, who popped a thumb in the air and had a big smile on his face.

When Xavier saw Shane later that day, he murmured, "Is everybody this helpful?"

"Yep." Shane didn't even look up.

"Do you even know what I'm talking about?"

"I heard about Ilse talking to you to devise a diet plan tailored for you," he shared. "And Dennis is quite concerned about your lack of nutrients. Every time I see you, you're packing one of those hefty green drinks." He looked up, saw it in his hand, and nodded. "Exactly."

"I'm not used to this," Xavier admitted.

"Well, get used to it," Shane replied. "A lot of good people are in the world. A lot of good people are where you came from as well. Still, to properly treat people, maybe they must be shown another way to heal the patient. That goes for the patients as well. You are seeing a new treatment plan here that obviously wasn't used at the last place you were at," he explained.

"Sure, but a special diet just for me?"

"It's not even a *special* diet," Shane clarified, cracking a smile as he faced Xavier. "Ilse is just dying to have something else to cook for somebody who will enjoy her food."

"The food's fantastic," Xavier shared, "but my digestive

system? Not so much."

"And yet it's complete, right? No surgeries?"

"Complete, yes. I believe so," he said cautiously. "The only surgery I had was to remove part of my small intestine. Even my broken leg and my broken arm were just reset and put in a cast. So no surgeries there either."

"So then what you really need for your digestion is a ton of supplementation, to get everything working properly," Shane recommended, "and, with any luck, that'll be something we can turn around fairly quickly."

"If you say so," he murmured.

Shane laughed. "I guess Hathaway House is quite a shock for you, isn't it?"

"It's a huge shock," Xavier declared, as he made his way to the floor to start one of Shane's sessions. "What I really want to do is walk and talk and have a full life, without everything giving me nausea."

"Is that the biggest thing in your life?"

"No. Obviously I have some physical injuries that need to heal. I'm coming out of that small intestine surgery. Of course my buddy and I got rattled pretty badly with that IED, so my joints are shot in my knees and my back. Yet nothing that surgery can fix. So I want to heal from my injuries and to strengthen my body again, but food's a big part of my problem too."

"Food's a huge part of healing," Shane confirmed, "and Dennis is onto part of that, but we will get you onto the other part of it as well. I'll talk to him about what's going into your shake. We should have you feeling better on the food level in maybe another week or so."

"Do you really think so? I've been dealing with this for months."

"Yep, I do think your stomach will be noticeably better in a week to ten days," he declared. "And if your upset stomach is holding you back because you need that set of nutrients, then we will do whatever we can to get them into you."

He winced at that. "I sure hope that doesn't mean injections. I hate needles."

"I have seen some of the biggest, baddest men in my life here, and they all hate needles." Shane chuckled. "It's something that never bothered me in my life growing up, but watching so many other people struggle with that phobia has been an interesting experience."

"Yeah, I wouldn't even say that it's that bad for me," Xavier clarified, "but it's definitely not something that I would want to deal with."

"Got it. So let's hope that you can sip on this shake throughout the day, without it coming back up again."

That was the hope.

Midmorning a couple days later, Xavier sat in his room, when Dennis appeared. Xavier eyed the shake in Dennis's hand. "It looks different."

"New combo of nutrients," Dennis announced, as he handed it to him. "Shane added in a few extra things for you."

"Good. Like what?" Xavier asked Dennis.

"Trace minerals, different bug treatment," Dennis explained. "And a butyric acid that helps heal the lining of your colon."

"All of it sounds good in theory," Xavier conceded, "but I really prefer to just eat real food."

"And you're getting there," Dennis noted.

"How do you know?" Xavier asked.

"Because I saw you get down some food today."

"I did, and so far it hasn't come up again yet," he shared cautiously. "It's a little early yet."

"Maybe, and, when you go for your rehab session, tell Shane that, so far, the food is staying down, and you don't want to do anything to bounce it back up again."

"But doesn't he have his own program to be worrying about?"

"If you can't keep down the healing and strengthening nutrients," Dennis stated, "you're not doing anyone's programs effectively. That would just set you back. We only aim for forward progress." And, with that, Dennis took off for the dining room again.

"Well, that looks like fun," Talia murmured as she entered Xavier's room and motioned toward the shake in his hand.

"Yeah, I'm drinking more than I'm eating these days," he shared, smiling at Talia. "How're you doing? I haven't seen you lately."

"Busy." She sighed. "Some days, some weeks, they're just really crazy busy," she murmured. "And these last few days have been a couple of them."

"And how's the yoga going?"

"Good." She brightened as she stared at him. "Matter of fact, very good. When are you coming?" she asked in a teasing voice.

"I wish, but I don't want to upchuck my dinner."

<h1 style="text-align:center">Chapter 5</h1>

TALIA LAUGHED AND then realized he wasn't joking. "Are you upchucking your food?" she asked in a sympathetic tone.

"Just once so far, since I've been here," he replied, "but, of course, once is bad enough."

"True, and it happens time and time again to patients here."

"Which doesn't make me feel any better at all."

She smiled. "No, of course not. Nobody wants to lose their cookies."

"Particularly when they are cookies," he said in mock horror.

Her laughter rang out. "I do love that sense of humor of yours," she stated, grinning broadly.

"Well then, I suggest that we spend some time having a cup of coffee together, though I'm not even sure I can hold that down."

"Sorry about that. Let's both have a green shake then."

"I live on these suckers," he muttered in a dark tone, staring at the one Dennis had just brought him. "I really want a steak and some veggies. Maybe a baked potato, but I'm pretty sure all of that'll be way too much."

"Have they mentioned to you about going with just single foods for a while?" she asked curiously.

"Actually Ilse told me that this morning during breakfast. And that she had a soup for me for lunch," he shared, as he looked out at the hot sun outside. "The trouble is, a hot soup isn't exactly what I would choose to eat today."

"Maybe not, but, if it comes from Ilse, I wouldn't turn it down."

He nodded. "And some salad would be good."

"Maybe just stick with that then, and don't add anything else to it," Talia suggested. "Buffets can be one of the problems. My family used to always go to buffets, and, every time I went, I would get sick. I blamed it on overeating. But then later I figured out that really it was more about a combination of so many different foods that my stomach couldn't handle it."

He nodded. "I have done that a couple times. I'm not too sure what's on the menu for today." He checked his watch. "It's not quite lunchtime yet, but I am a little bit hungry."

"In that case, let's go," she said, bouncing to her feet. "If you're hungry, you need to eat."

"But it might not be time yet."

"It depends on what Ilse's got prepped for you. Let's go take a look."

XAVIER HESITATED.

"I know. You don't want to be a bother," Talia muttered, with an eye roll.

"Everybody is doing so much, and I feel so appreciated," Xavier admitted, "but I also feel as if I'm being a spoiled jerk." She burst out laughing again, and he had to grin. "You might think I have a sense of humor," he began, "but I crack more jokes around you just because I love to hear your laughter."

She stopped laughing and stared at him. "I think that's the nicest thing I've heard somebody say to me in a very long time."

"What? Is everybody here blind? You're gorgeous," he said, "but that smile? For me that trumps looks anytime."

She chuckled. "Come on then. Trust me in this. We'll go to the dining room and see if you can eat right away whatever is available, even if just a little bit," she suggested. "If you're hungry, I firmly believe that you need to eat while you have an appetite."

"Maybe. Still, it's hard for me."

"And just because it's hard for you doesn't mean it's not worth doing," she replied.

He rolled his eyes at that. "Does that line work for you?"

"It's been working for me for a while," she stated, "so you can't break my streak now."

He allowed himself to be tugged toward the dining room. When she popped in and saw Dennis, she shared, "Well a miracle's occurred."

He looked at her, saw Xavier beside her, and asked, "What's that?"

"He has a little bit of an appetite." She smiled.

"A little bit," Xavier repeated.

But Dennis had a beaming smile and nodded. "What's your fancy? Protein? Veggies?

Xavier said, "I want to try a small salad."

"Done," Dennis declared. "Go sit down."

Chapter 6

UNFORTUNATELY, XAVIER'S STOMACH didn't seem to like dinner, or the breakfast the next day or dinner that night, or for several days. Talia started to get really worried, as she watched the weight fall off him. As was her practice, she came to visit him before lunch.

He gave her a wan smile. "Yeah, apparently they just did some cultures, and I've got a tummy bug," he shared, with a frown. "Not sure where I got that from."

But her relief was overwhelming. "Yes, while it might be terrible, it isn't devastating. Plus, that is fixable."

He nodded. "At least that's the hope." He grinned at her. "Maybe by the time I get the okay to eat again, I can get the okay to gain a whole pile of weight too. I tell you that Dennis seems to be chomping at the bit to fatten me up."

She nodded. "And honestly, I'm in his camp. You've lost a lot of weight."

"I don't think it's a *lot* of weight," he clarified. "Definitely a few pounds though. Still, being injured, not moving around much, not holding down most of my food, I can't seem to put on any weight."

"You were very slim when you arrived," she noted, "but now I have to admit you're kinda gaunt-looking." He frowned at her. She frowned right back and added, "No, I'm not saying you're ugly or anything else." She chuckled at that. "However, I'll be happy when you're back to eating and regaining some of that lost weight."

"Maybe after antibiotics for ten days, heavy supplements of good bacteria and enzymes, and *blah, blah, blah,*" he shared, with a hand wave.

"Right, so more shakes?"

"Definitely shakes for the next few days and only soft foods," he said. "And only if I can keep them down."

"That would be the first criteria, I would think," she confirmed, with a bright smile. "I would suggest we go have coffee."

He shook his head. "Honestly, coffee isn't even sitting well."

"How long until they expect you to start feeling better?"

He shrugged. "Three to four days."

"Okay, that's doable," she murmured.

"Says you." He glared at her. "I'll be really cranky without my coffee."

She gave him a flat stare. "No cranks allowed."

He groaned. "Caffeine is a necessity."

"No, it's just in your mind," she told him.

"Yeah, *right,*" he muttered. "My mind is pretty decisive." And he gave her a big fat smile with that to belie the fact that he wasn't upset.

"How about a cuppa tea?" she asked. "A little weak, clear, so no milk or sugar."

He frowned. "I've never really been a tea drinker."

"Maybe it's a good time to try it," she murmured, "because it is caffeine. So, if you get a caffeine-withdrawal headache, tea might stave it off."

"We could try."

"Good. How about we take it outside though?"

He looked out the window in his room but hesitated.

"Let's go outside," she said, "maybe in the wheelchair because you're not looking all that hot." He glared at her, but she shrugged. "Just calling a spade a spade. Goes along with that *being skinny* look."

He growled. "I'm not skinny."

"You're past skinny," she murmured, but he went to the wheelchair obediently. And she noticed that. "Obviously you're not feeling very well because that wasn't much of a protest."

"Just weak," he said. "And I don't want to wipe out and have to rely on you to get me back."

"I wouldn't even try," she declared. "I would get two orderlies."

He chuckled at that. "Might not be the worst idea in the world to do that either. It's good that you have orderlies here. I also understand animals are here."

"Yep, Stan's got kittens, if you want to go see them."

"Stan's a mama cat?" he asked. "Who would name a female cat *Stan*?"

She chuckled. "Nope, nope, nope, nope. Stan's the vet, and he's got kittens, and the mama got hit by a car and needed surgery. So they're looking after her babies down there until she recovers, probably bottle-feeding them."

He stared at her. "Good Lord. I would love to see them."

"Let's go take a look then. We can always go for a walk outside, and, when we come back, if you think you're up for it, we can try a cuppa tea."

"Sounds like a full afternoon. Aren't you doing something today?"

"It's Saturday," she said cheerfully. "And I'm not doing

anything."

"Wow, I've lost track of my days just because of not doing so well," he murmured.

"That's what happens," she noted. "All your programs came to a complete stop because you weren't strong enough to follow them."

He winced. "I sure hope I don't stay down for long," he muttered. "I have only so much time to get through this."

"And don't you start worrying about that either," she said, pointing a finger at him. "What about Zander? Did you update him?"

"No, I figured there was no point in making him worry. He is doing better though."

"Good," she said. "Has he applied?"

"He has, and has been put on a waitlist."

"You might want to put in a good word for him with Dani."

"If that'll make a difference, absolutely," he declared.

"I'm not sure if it'll make any difference," she replied. "I know we often have a long waitlist. But other things have to line up too, such as, Zander has to pass a bunch of tests. His doctors at that end have to sign off on his transfer papers too."

Downstairs, Xavier was introduced to the ladies who ran the office of the vet clinic, and then Robin came out, holding kittens. She smiled at him and asked, "After these guys by any chance, are you?"

Immediately he held out his arms, and she dropped two tiny sleepy little guys in his arms, and Xavier held them up against his chest.

"They've just been fed," she shared, "so they're looking for a warm place to snuggle up."

"Wow," he whispered, as he stared down at the two Persians. "They're so tiny."

"How's the mama cat doing?" Talia asked.

"Hopefully she'll make it. She's got a broken back leg, and she's pretty bruised up. However, with any luck, she'll come through this like a trooper," she explained. "We do keep the kittens with her most of the time, but we can't have them on her all the time until she's a little bit better. So we're trying to keep them close enough that they know that that's mom but not slow her healing either."

He nodded at that. "You're blessed to work with them. I don't think I could handle the accidents and putting them down."

Robin nodded. "There is a certain poignancy in working with animals," she said. "I don't think I could do the job upstairs," she noted, with a smile over at Talia.

"It's different," Talia murmured. "It seems down here you get the decision between life and death more often."

"We do, and sometimes it weighs on us," she admitted. "Sometimes Stan gets pretty overwrought when he sees perfectly healthy dogs that have either been abused or have a disease that could have been prevented if they'd received proper care. Of course the only decent option is to put them down." She shook her head. "We try not to focus on that. Just like you try to focus on healing upstairs, we try to focus on healing down here."

"The kittens are absolutely adorable," he whispered, dropping a gentle kiss on the head of one of them. It was so small that it was hard to even imagine how it could survive. Finally he picked them up and held them back up to Robin. "Thank you for that," he said.

Her tone was sincere, and her smile warm, as she nodded. "Anytime you need to touch some of the gentler sides of Mother Nature, come on down. We always have some animals here."

"And I'm glad to hear that," Xavier replied. "I've seen some of the guys having a few dogs upstairs. I wasn't exactly sure what the deal was."

"Dogs and cats," Robin confirmed. "They're what we class as therapy animals. Plus, we have Hoppers, a huge rabbit. We keep them here full-time. They live on Hathaway House property, and some of them are in better shape than others. So please never feed them. Racer in particular—which is the little guy, the Chihuahua with wheels—as his stomach is definitely touchy."

"Well, he gets my sympathies then," Xavier noted, with feeling, "because that's definitely my problem too."

At that, Robin chuckled. "And, with Ilse's cooking, that can't be easy to turn down any of her food."

"No, it isn't," he complained. "I would absolutely love to tank up on some of that awesome food." He asked her, "Do you get to eat the dining room food?"

"As employees, we can, but not necessarily," Robin replied. "I have a partner, so we tend to eat together as much as possible."

He nodded. "I get that too. A special someone is something else that I don't have."

"Hey, stick around here long enough," Robin said cheerfully, "and you'll probably end up with somebody."

He looked at her in surprise. "Sorry?"

She smiled. "A whole lot of matchmaking goes on at this center in the last few years," she shared. "It's amazing the number of partners who have hooked up." She looked over at Talia. "You escaped all that, didn't you?"

"Well, if *escape* is the right word, yes," Talia replied, "but you met your boyfriend here. It's Lance, right?"

Robin smiled a beaming smile. "I met Iain and Lance here. Now I'm with Iain, and Jessica is with Lance." She pointed to Xavier. "Ooh, that's someone you should meet. Lance is setting up a center for veterans trying to transition into life after rehab," she explained. "So, if you have any issues trying to figure out what you're doing next in your life, you can always give Lance a call."

He frowned at her. "Somebody from Hathaway is doing that?"

"He was a former patient here at the center, and now he's recovered and helping other patients to find their next step in life."

"I should definitely talk to him," Xavier admitted. "I'm really not sure what I'm doing after rehab."

"And you don't need to worry about it right now either," Robin pointed out. "Just like any of the animals down here and any of you guys upstairs, you need to focus first on healing and growing the way you need to. After that you can deal with finding the right occupation for you."

And, with that, they left her and headed outside. The heat of the sun beat down on them.

Talia suggested, "Let's head to the trees. It'll be much nicer there." She pushed Xavier's wheelchair off to the left and around a pathway that took them directly into the trees.

As soon as they were in the shade, he sighed. "I love Texas, love the heat, but wow."

"I love the sun too, but the heat is a wow for me also," she murmured. "We are so spoiled because we have air-conditioning all the time that I forget what it's really like out here."

"And yet it's gorgeous," he murmured. Off in the distance he watched a woman working with clippers on a couple trees. "Even have women landscapers out here," he noted, amazed.

"That's Bella, and she runs the team of landscapers," Talia clarified, with a smile. "Not everybody here just does clerical work or nursing."

"Hey, I didn't mean it that way," he said. "Yard work is just a very taxing physical job."

"Yep, and she works hard at it. I don't think I could do that job," Talia murmured.

"If it's not where your heart is, it makes sense not to do the job," he noted. "When you think about it, it's all about doing what you love."

"If that's an option, yes," she agreed. She looked down at him. "And what about you? What do you love?"

"Well, I loved the navy," he shared. "And I could potentially go back and do a desk job, if I wanted it."

"And you could probably find another job too," she suggested, "that wasn't necessarily a desk job."

"Maybe, but moving from the job I used to do to a desk position would always feel like a consolation prize."

"I think we all have more than just one dream job," she shared.

WORDS TO LIVE by, and ones Xavier thought about for a long time after their walk. He sat in his room, waiting for dinnertime, wondering if it was safe to even try real food.

A little bit later he was in his wheelchair and heading to the dining room.

Dennis looked up and greeted him. "Well, today is the day. Are you ready to try something?"

Xavier nodded. "But I want to stick with something easy."

"How about with a baked potato?" Dennis suggested. "Nice, simple trimmings if you want them. Other than that, stick to just the baked potato with some butter."

"That might not be a bad idea," Xavier said. "Yet it's not quite what I had in mind."

"Of course not, but rice and potato can be some of the easiest things to digest."

"Okay, let's give it a try. Do I get to have anything on it?"

"Other than butter, maybe a little bit of sour cream but don't go too heavy on that, as fat can be hard to digest."

"Right," he murmured. "Okay, let's try the baked potato."

As he sat down to eat, he loved the smell and wondered just how long he would have to be on bland, easy-to-digest foods. And yet it was still way better than nothing at all or just green shakes.

And almost with that thought, Shane showed up with a big green shake again, placing it before Xavier. "Courtesy of Dennis," he said, yet looking at the potato approvingly. "That's the way to start, nice and easy."

"It's a little hard when you're getting steak," Xavier grumbled in disgust.

Shane chuckled. "And that may be, but no point in giving you a steak if it's not staying down."

"I know. Just one of those things I have to put up with for a while again."

"It absolutely is, and we're sorry that you can't eat just

any food. However, as soon as you can, you're welcome to tuck in."

"And I will as soon as I get there," he said, staring down at the potato. "It does look good."

"Actually it looks freaking awesome," Shane replied. "I think I'll go get one myself." And, with that, he took off.

Meanwhile Xavier tucked in. It wasn't long before he had the entire potato down. So far, so good. His stomach was holding strong. Now if only it would hold for the rest of the evening. In the interim, he would sip away at his green shake.

By the time he went to bed that night, he felt pretty decent.

When he woke up the next morning he was even further emboldened. So, when he headed down for breakfast, he looked over at Dennis with a big smile on his face.

"So it was good?" Dennis asked.

"It was very good," Xavier declared. "No stomach pains at all."

"Good to hear."

Xavier looked over the food in front of him but frowned.

Dennis suggested, "How about just some scrambled eggs?"

Of course Xavier was looking at everything else, and he sighed. "I guess I should stay with gentle foods, *huh*?"

"Absolutely," Dennis agreed. "The last thing we want is to set you back right now."

"Okay, scrambled eggs it is."

And with a decent plateful of scrambled eggs and a plain piece of toast, he headed out to the deck. He chose a spot in the early morning sun, wondering how any place could be so stunningly beautiful. With the rolling hills and the horses out here, it was just postcard perfect. He caught sight of Dani, standing against the deck railing. "I don't know how you managed it," he called out to her, "but it's really beautiful."

She turned and smiled at him. "Well, I think somebody above"—she pointed to the skies—"had something to do with that."

He chuckled. "Absolutely, but what you've accomplished here is pretty impressive."

She smiled, obviously pleased. "Thanks, it's been a labor of love. If you ever see my father around here—he's the older gentleman with the big impressive moustache—it was all built for him."

Xavier nodded at her. "I think I've seen him around. The Major?"

She nodded. "That's my father. He was in worse shape than you when he came back from a mission," she shared. "And his depression was something else, and his physical state was even worse. He was suicidal, and his whole world had collapsed. It took us a long time to get him back to decent health, mentally and physically. During that process, the idea for this place became a reality, more to help him than to help anybody else," she murmured. "Of course all good things tend to spread."

"You're not kidding," Xavier agreed, looking at her with additional respect. "And that's even more impressive to think that you did it for your father."

She smiled. "He's the only family I have, so I wasn't prepared to lose him quite yet," she murmured.

"Understood. I hope he understands how lucky he is."

"Well, you can always remind him anytime," she said, with a chuckle. "I'm sure he would appreciate that." Xavier grinned at her, as she gave a small wave and added, "I have to head back to the office now."

And he began to realize just how much work went into running this place. It was pretty crazy. He couldn't imagine what kind of dedication it would have taken originally to get this idea off the ground, but knowing that it was for her own father, that made it very understandable. And he meant it when he told her how it was even more impressive because too often people just wrung their hands together and didn't know what to do and, therefore, didn't do anything.

Whereas she'd buckled in, and she'd helped create something very impressive that not only was a benefit for him, but also for so many others here as well. And then realized that he'd just missed his opportunity to ask about Zander's application. He turned to see if Dani was still around, but she was long gone. He groaned. "That was foolish."

"What was foolish?" asked a woman with a cheerful voice.

His smile immediately brightened as he turned to face her. "Talia, I was hoping I would see you."

"See? We're back to that honesty again. I really like that."

He laughed. "With somebody like you, it's always best to be honest. You would see through the lies in a heartbeat."

"And why would you want to lie to me anyway?" she asked, with a bright smile. "The world has enough problems without lying to people."

"I don't like lying either," he shared. "Particularly when you find yourself in this situation where a lot of the issues are medical. They don't exactly tell you the truth. They just skirt around it, saying nothing."

She nodded. "You're not the first person to mention

that. I think being straightforward is always best, but not everybody wants to or is ready to hear the unvarnished truth," she murmured.

"No, I guess not," he conceded, "but, in my case, it's definitely what I would prefer."

"Good, I'll keep that in mind."

He nodded. "You do that. I think relationships are always better off with honesty anyway."

"Oh, I agree," she confirmed. "I think it's the biggest breakdown between people when that lack of communication and honesty comes up."

"Good then," he replied, "we're on the same page with that too." He flashed her a bright smile and added, "I managed to keep dinner down last night."

Her face split with joy. "That's wonderful news," she declared, as she sat down. "I can't think of anything better."

"I just had some eggs, so I'm really hoping …"

"I am too," she murmured. "I am too."

Chapter 7

A S IT WAS, it seemed as if Xavier had turned a corner. Every day he appeared to get a little bit more color in his face and a little bit stronger. His stomach also seemed to have calmed down to the point that he was capable of eating more and more. In fact, mealtimes were a joy for him now. And Talia knew for a fact that Dennis was in his element. Even Ilse came out at almost every meal to check on Xavier. He was embarrassed and flustered by all the attention and yet at the same time amazed that people cared. Talia often just sat here with him, his plate full, while she watched him work his way through whatever meal he had. And he no longer protested what they offered to him. He didn't say anything. He just sat down and ate it, as if finally confident that whatever they gave him was in his best interests.

Several days later, after many meals had worked through his system as they should, he finally put down his fork and gave her a beaming smile. "Food's never tasted this good."

"What?" she asked in mock astonishment. "Is that coming from you? You who doesn't care about food?"

"Hey," he protested, "I didn't know it could be like this."

"Apparently your stomach didn't either," she murmured.

He nodded. "Isn't that something too," he noted. "It's hard to imagine just what a joy it is to be eating again.

Without cramps and a million other things that we won't discuss at the dinner table," he added, with a smile.

"Oh, I'm pretty sure I've heard it all by now," she murmured, chuckling.

He nodded. "I'm sure you have. Doesn't mean I want you to be regaled with way more of it."

At that, she laughed. "Don't worry about it. It's all good. As long as you're eating, and it's staying down, everybody here is thrilled for you."

He nodded. "And who thought, who knew, that the cure would be something simple."

"Well, it's never that simple, not until you figure it out," she noted. "Think about it. People spend lifetimes going through pain and indigestion and never really realizing what is the problem. They're quite content to think that they've just got a tummy ache."

"Yeah, but when the tummy ache hits me like that?" He shuddered.

"Exactly," she murmured. "You're doing a ton better now."

"Yeah," he agreed, "and it's pretty hard not to appreciate the fact that everybody here worked so hard to get me back on track. Between the doctors and Shane and Ilse and Dennis, it feels as if it were a community effort." He laughed. "And isn't that something?"

"As I told you before, we all care," she reminded him. "You're not a number. You're not a patient. You're somebody to us."

"And that's the difference," he said. "I get it. I just never expected to see that."

"I think it's a shame that our world has come down to number-crunching to the extent that most patients don't understand that they deserve more," she murmured.

"I don't even know if it's that so much," he clarified, "but maybe more about just knowledge of the science of the body. We don't always understand just what we need and what we could use." He explained, "It goes back to that theory about you don't know what you don't know. And when you don't know something, how are you ever supposed to know that you don't know it?"

She blinked. It took her a moment, and then she laughed. "That's very true."

"Exactly. Glad you understood that." And he grinned at her.

There was just something about him—the smiles, the grace with which he finally accepted that people here cared—that made her sit up and take notice of him. The trouble was, she was sitting up and taking notice of him probably more than she should. She sighed at that point.

"Ooh," Xavier said, "that didn't sound good."

She looked at him. "Why?"

"That just sounded like a real heavy-weather kinda sigh."

"It wasn't intended that way," she protested.

"Are you sure?" he asked. "It sounded as if, *I've got the world on my shoulders, and I don't know how to fix it.*"

"Well, for one," she began, "if the whole world is on your or my shoulders, it's not for you or me to fix."

He stared at her and then laughed. "Good point. I'm fine with that too."

She smiled. "It's amazing, when you think about it. So much in life is open-ended, and we have options, and then so much in life seems as if we have zero choice at all."

He nodded. "I feel that sometimes too. No, not some-times," he corrected, "but all the time recently, or at least in the months before I arrived here. It seemed as if, no matter the problem, nothing could be done. I was watching Zander get worse and worse, every time he caught the next thing. It was just … heartbreaking because I couldn't help him."

"I'm glad that you decided to come here and that you're helping Zander get here too."

"I'm glad I decided to come as well, but more so now because Zander is pulling through."

"Did you ever talk to Dani about getting Zander here?"

He shook his head. "And I had a perfect opportunity just a few days ago, and I blew it."

"There is no such thing as blowing things with Dani," Talia pointed out. "She's very approachable."

"I know, but I feel as if the stars and the moon and all the astrological signs must line up so that she'll give me the answer I want to hear."

Talia frowned at him. "You really do think the world's against you, don't you?"

"Sometimes it seems that way," he stated darkly. "You know when you want the answer that you want from a doctor, but you're afraid to ask because you just know it'll be the wrong answer?"

She nodded. "I think that's fear talking."

"Sure, it's all fear," he agreed, "but fear is something that's very hard to walk away from."

"It hasn't really been much of an issue in my world," she shared, "so I'll just have to accept that, for you, unfortunately the fear's been part of your day-to-day life."

"It has been when you wake up after an injury like mine," he shared. "The worst part was lying out there with part of the vehicle on top of me, yet knowing that Zander, beside me, was worse off. And, even though I tried calling out to him, I just couldn't rouse him. He survived with a broken pelvis, both legs broken, plus several ribs. My injuries were almost as bad, as one of my legs was crushed and the other broken, plus an arm. But, in both cases, we survived with our lives, so it's all good."

She looked over at him and winced. "I'm sorry. I didn't realize you were both in the same accident."

He nodded. "Same unit, same set of training missions, same vehicle, same IED. There were just so many of them," he whispered. "And you never really think it'll happen to you, until it does, and then you wonder why life did that to you. Still, it's easy to forget about all the other guys who were affected just as badly too."

"I don't think you can ever spread your energy to all the rest of the guys," she suggested. "I think you get to a point where you have to focus on you and only you to heal. That's one of the reasons why I'm glad you came, even if Zander wasn't ready to be moved yet. I would love to see Zander here too, but you must focus on you."

"And I am. It's just that I want good things for him too."

"So let's go talk to Dani," she suggested.

He looked at her. "What do you mean, both of us?"

"Sure, why not? Dani doesn't scare me." And she twinkled a smile back at him.

"Well, she doesn't scare me either, but she's intimidating."

"She's not intimidating, but the situation might be intimidating."

"You're splitting hairs," he said.

"Not trying to," Talia replied. "Yet I know this is really important. I'm just trying to point out that Dani isn't an ogre. If she can accommodate somebody, she will."

"But why would she accommodate Zander if she's already turned him down?"

"But did she turn him down, or was it more that he's not ready yet or maybe Dani didn't have a free bed? Or was it, hey, Zander needs to get well and be in a better state of health before we move him."

"I don't know," Xavier admitted. "I didn't see the file, didn't see the answer."

"So maybe that's one of the things to clarify first."

He hesitated, then nodded. "It feels as if I need to talk to her."

"Then talk to her. Just accept that Dani is a good person and tell her about Zander. She's not scary."

He looked over at Talia and made a face. "She might not be scary to you, but she's kinda scary to the rest of us."

Talia burst out laughing. "Maybe, but she would be surprised to hear it. Still, she's also a really good person, so I wouldn't worry about it too much."

"Says you," he muttered. Then he smiled and nodded. "I'll get around to it. Zander isn't ready yet."

"No, but you might want to get his name on the list first anyway."

"I understand," he said.

Just then Dani popped up in the dining room and looked over at him. "Hey, how's the stomach?"

"Much better." Then he called out, "Hey, Dani, you got a minute?"

"Sure," she said, walking over with her plate. "Mind if I join you?"

"No, not at all," he said, with a glance over at Talia. "A friend of mine who's applied to come here," he began, "actually he applied well before me, and he's had a lot of health complications, and apparently he was turned down."

She studied him. "Interesting," she murmured. "We don't turn down very many people."

"That's what Talia was saying. So I don't know if it was a case of *turned down* or he needed something more or it just wasn't the right time. … Maybe you had a waitlist."

"We always have a waitlist now. What's his name?" she asked.

"Zander Tolston. He's a really nice guy. We've been in and out of missions together for most of our adult life," he explained. "I know he had pneumonia when I left, but he's pulling out of it now."

"Ah," she murmured. "I think that was more about we had a bed for him at the time, but he didn't have permission."

"Permission?" Xavier pounced. "What does that mean?"

"Doctor's permission to travel, to be without his supervision, whatever it is. We still have a lot of bureaucracy to go through," she murmured, as she eyed him. "Now if he's physically better and he's more capable of traveling at this point, then that might be something that can be looked at again. Has he resubmitted an application?"

"I thought he told me that earlier. Yet I don't know for sure. Maybe he assumed he would be on a waitlist."

She frowned at that. "I'll look it up, but a resubmission on his part shows that he is still interested."

"I'm pretty sure he won't have a problem doing that, if he hasn't already," he murmured.

"Let me know," Dani replied, "and, when I get back to the office, I'll take a look."

Xavier smiled. "Thank you." As soon as Dani was gone,

Xavier let out a *whoosh*.

Talia smiled at him and asked, "See? Was that so scary?"

"No," he admitted. "I figured I better grab the bull by the horns and see what's up. Then at least maybe I can tell Zander whenever he's healthy and able to travel that maybe we could make this happen."

"Exactly," she replied, with a bright smile. "It doesn't have to be all bad news. And just because it deals with your friend doesn't mean that everything will automatically go badly."

"No, but so many things have gone wrong for this guy that I feel somebody put a target on his back. Zander's just been *it* for so long."

"Maybe this time being *it* will be a good thing," she suggested gently. "Give Dani a chance to check, see what's going on. That'll give you the inside scoop on it, and then you can contact Zander, tell him to resubmit, and see what else might need to happen."

"I'll do that," he stated, with a bright smile. "And thanks, by the way."

She frowned. "Thanks for what?"

"For giving me the courage to try." He laughed.

"You didn't need courage," she noted. "I get the feeling you'll walk through fire for your friends."

"For this one in particular, yes, as he saved my life."

"During the accident?"

"No, before. We were up against a sniper, and he took him out after I'd been shot. The sniper was coming up for a kill shot, and Zander took him down."

"Nice. Well, nice for you. Not so nice for the sniper."

"And that's the way it is," he muttered, his tone darkening. "It seems as if somebody's always doing better, and somebody has to do worse in order to make that happen."

"Sorry to hear that for you guys out there who were in the thick of things," she said, "but it's a whole new world out there now, with plenty of happiness and success and healing to go around. Yet so many people can't even begin to understand what you've been through." She added, "That's one of the reasons why you might want to make friends around here because they do understand."

"I know," he admitted, "but I guess I've also been reticent to get into that whole tale-sharing thing because it just drags up so much other stuff. It was always something that I could count on Zander for."

"Counting on Zander's great, when he's here. But you do seem a little bit lost without him."

He looked at her and protested, "I haven't had a chance to be lost. Just so much is going on since I got here—and not that long ago either—that that's hardly a fair assessment."

"Maybe not *lost*," she conceded, "but it feels as if you're missing Zander a lot."

He gave her a bright smile. "That is true. I have been, but honestly, you've been great, and I really appreciate your friendship."

"Hey, our friendship is a whole different story. That's because I like you. Not because we shared a major attack." And, with that, she got a reminder *ping* from her phone. Looking at her watch, she shook her head. "And I have to go to work."

As she got up, she smiled at him. "I'll see you later." And took off.

XAVIER WAS DELIGHTED that his stomach and digestive system seemed to improve, slowly at first but then stronger and stronger, until he was testing out different meats, different vegetables, different starches. At the end of the evening he could always tell whether he was doing well or would spend half the night sitting in the bathroom. Not his favorite occupation, given where he was at and what the next day would bring.

Shane could always tell from the look on his face the next morning how he'd done overnight. But eventually Shane got to the point of just glancing at him and then carrying on.

Several weeks later Xavier shared, "I haven't had a bout of digestive issues in a quite a while now."

"And that is huge news," Shane declared. "I don't know if you've noticed, but you have put on some weight. And we're all very grateful to see it."

Xavier nodded. "Probably about five pounds."

Shane snorted. "I would say it's closer to twenty."

"Oh, I don't think it's that much," Xavier argued, "but I could see maybe ten. But let's do a base weight right now." He hopped on a nearby scale and was quite surprised. "Well, it was between our estimates. Thirteen pounds up."

"A lovely sign," Shane said, with a nod. "Another few pounds and we might get into building muscle again."

"Why not now?"

"Because you're still healing. And we can't have your body expending too much energy in the wrong direction."

That made sense. Xavier just hated that everything was being held back.

Shane obviously read his mind and murmured, "Don't worry about it. Once you're back to full strength, and we're not wasting away all that lovely energy again, you'll jump forward—and faster than you would expect."

"It doesn't seem like it now," he grumbled.

Shane chuckled at that. "Being eager to see progress is always a good sign."

"Is anybody ever here who isn't eager to see progress?"

Shane nodded. "We probably don't see that very often, but we do have people here who want to stay. They don't have anything else waiting for them. They don't have a life that they enjoy yet. They get catered to here in a certain way, and sometimes we see their progress stalls because they really don't want to move forward to the next stage of their life."

Xavier frowned at Shane. "I hadn't even considered that. I just want to see myself back to good health again and as strong as I can be."

"And a lot of people want that as well, but they also get mixed up with what their future really looks like, and they aren't ready for it."

Xavier sat down on the mat beside Shane and shook his head. "The things that we get messed up with."

"Well, you're still messed up dealing with your friend. You want him here, but he's not here. So in some ways I was a little worried that you wouldn't progress yourself."

"I don't think that should be a problem," Xavier stated. "I just want to ensure my buddy gets an equal chance to be as well as he can be."

"And Dani is looking into his application. It was brought up during one of our recent meetings."

Xavier looked over at Shane. "Wow, I'm really glad to hear that."

"Hey, we care here," Shane said, with a smile.

"And I get that. I hadn't really seen how much of a difference that kind of caring could make, but I do now."

"Good. First things first though, is you have to look after you. You are of no value to your friend if you can't get yourself cleaned up."

"And here I thought I was doing so much better."

"You *are* doing much better," Shane murmured, "but it's not quite good enough."

Xavier glared at him. "Now you'll tell me that I'm not doing enough after telling me that we couldn't even progress because we needed to slow down."

"Oh no. I think now that we're getting your digestive system cleaned up," he explained, "we'll have great progress physically. I'm not sure about emotionally."

"Wow," Xavier muttered. "Are we back to my friend again?"

"I don't know. Are we? It definitely feels as if something is holding you back."

That surprised Xavier. He shook his head. "I don't think so," he replied cautiously.

"Good," Shane stated, his tone serious, as he gave Xavier a straightforward look. "Because, if there is anything, *anything* that's making you insecure, feel bad or in some way … stopping you from progressing, then we need to know about it. We need to nip it in the bud fast. Your time here is at a premium, and we want you to get the most value from what you do here."

"And what is it that I could possibly be worrying about?" he asked.

"You tell me," Shane replied.

That was one thing about Shane. He never evaded a hard topic. It's almost as if he had some more psychology courses under his belt than most of the physical therapists.

Xavier frowned at him and shrugged.

"So let's discuss your friend then," Shane suggested.

Xavier winced. "You think it's all back to Zander?"

"I have no idea," Shane admitted. "I just feel as if maybe you gained a certain amount of relief when having these abdominal pains, when everything was slowed down."

Xavier felt his anger shooting to life inside him. "That's not fair," he said. "You were the ones that made everything come to a stop until this healed."

"Exactly, but I'm also seeing a certain amount of *Okay, good, that will maybe give Zander time to catch up with me.*"

At that Xavier flushed, a dull angry flush, and shook his head. "That's not fair," he snapped. "That's not something I would do."

"I'm not sure you're consciously doing it," Shane pointed out, "as much as it's a subconscious wish. You two were close, always close, and, in every step of this way, of this journey, you've been pretty well neck and neck, except that you got to come here, and your buddy got sick."

Xavier nodded slowly. "Sure, but I won't hold back my own progress because Zander got sick."

"Are you sure?" Shane asked. "Because I heard rumors that you wouldn't even come here until Zander was better."

He flushed at that too. He stared at Shane, feeling a dull anger inside. "This conversation is over," he declared, with a wave of his hand. "Either we're doing a workout today or I'm going back to my room."

"Then talk to me or go back to your room," Shane said calmly. "Your choice."

Xavier glared at him, struggled back in his wheelchair, and pushed his way out of the room. Such an emotional vibration ran through him that, for a moment, he wondered whether he was okay or he could possibly have a heart attack. Xavier had such a tight feeling around his chest that it scared him. He didn't even know what to think anymore.

Back in his room, he shut the door with a little more force than was necessary and crawled back up onto his bed. If he needed to stay here for another bloody day, he would. But he would not take any more of that nonsense. They had no reason to even start talking to him like that. He'd never done anything to deserve it, and no way was Xavier holding back because of Zander. And, with that, he shut out the outside world and kept it at bay.

Chapter 8

TALIA DIDN'T SEE Xavier at lunch, and neither did she see him as she headed down for dinner. It was an unusual pattern, but, when she saw Shane, she sensed something was off. "What's going on?" she asked.

He gave her a lopsided smile. "Just some hard truths that somebody doesn't want to look at."

"Xavier?"

He nodded slowly. "Have you seen him today?"

She shook her head. "No, I haven't. Did he not show up for your session?"

"He showed up, but he turned and wheeled out about ten minutes later," he shared. "Didn't like what I had to say."

She stared at him in shock. "That's too bad because he was doing much better."

"He *was* doing much better, better enough that I thought it was time that I brought up something else."

"Okay. Would you care to share?" When he hesitated, she nodded. "That's fine. You don't have to tell me anything. I understand that his medical records are private."

"And I'm not even sure that it's as much private," he added, "as Xavier's having some things to work through, and I think he needs to do that on his own."

"Can he though?" she asked, as she stepped up to get

served for dinner.

"That'll be the question, whether he can find his way through this maze on his own or whether he needs to get help. Then, if he needs help, will he ask for it?"

She winced at that. "Asking for help seems to be such a stumbling block for so many of the patients here."

"For some, and then it can be the absolute opposite for others."

"So true. I guess you see it all here, don't you?"

"Sometimes I think I've seen it all, and then something new happens that I haven't seen. I continuously get surprised by the way that some of us process our emotions and the way some don't."

"I wonder if I should go talk to him?"

"You could try. I suspect that he won't let you in."

"Have you gone to see him?"

"Nope, I haven't," Shane stated, with a grin. "I walked past his room, and the door's quite firmly shut."

"Oh, *great*," she muttered. "That's a stage I'm not sure I'm ready for."

"You mean, being shut out?" He nodded. "I have to tell you, almost everybody here goes through it at one stage or another."

"Doesn't make me feel any better," she muttered.

He looked over at her. "So how serious is it between you guys?"

"I've only known him a few weeks," she noted, with a shrug, "so how serious can it be?"

"Here? It can get deep very quickly," he stated. "The problems we deal with here end up wiping out all that time that you would normally have spent in getting to know each other," he explained. "Not only are you under a time frame here, but the issues are something that so many relationships never even have to deal with. How often do you see somebody go through a major trauma and have to be there to help support them? Here at Hathaway House, you find out who they are right away."

"Maybe," she conceded, "yet they also have to figure out who they are, and that's not the easiest because they haven't had any chance to figure it out either, not with all the surgeries and healing time and rehab."

"And that is also a truth that makes this a very unique place," Shane agreed, "so, I wish you the best."

She shrugged. "I'm not even sure what I want for myself or for him. Obviously I want him to get better and to have a wonderful, successful life after this rehab process," she shared. "Yet I've never really been in this position before. … Sometimes I wonder if I could even handle a relationship with somebody like him."

"Which at least tells me that it's serious enough that you are thinking about it." She glared at him. He just smiled. "The fact that you are thinking about it is good. … The fact that he's dealing with his stuff right now is also good."

"But *is* he dealing with it?" she asked worriedly. "Or is he just hiding away and trying to ignore it?"

"Either way it's for him to sort out," Shane stated firmly. "If I don't see him anytime soon, then I will go to his room and check on him."

"The nurses will do that anyway, right?" she asked, a note of worry in her tone.

"Absolutely, the rounds still continue. The medications will be handed out. He will be checked and confirmed that he's alive, if that's what you're thinking."

"It's partly what I'm thinking, but I wouldn't go that far.

So thanks for putting that thought in my head."

Shane burst out laughing. "We haven't lost anybody in that way here."

"No, not yet," she muttered, "and it's the *yet* part that bothers me."

"Then maybe after dinner, stop in and see how he is."

"And if he won't let me in?"

"Then he's not ready to deal with this," Shane replied gently. "And sometimes the best thing you can do is just walk away."

She decided not to stop in after dinner because Xavier's door was definitely closed, and she got this really weird feeling. But the next morning she went straight to his room, after worrying about him all night, and knocked. When there was no answer, she knocked again.

"Go away," he said.

She frowned at that, shook her head, opened the door, and popped her head inside. "No, I won't go away. I don't know what's going on, but I worry terribly about you. I even texted you, but you didn't answer."

He frowned at her, pulled out his phone, and muttered, "I didn't see it. … Sorry about that."

She nodded, feeling better about it, took a step inside. "You coming down for breakfast?"

"No."

"Is your stomach upset again?" she asked. "Do you want me to send Shane up?" Immediately he glared at her, and she stopped. "Okay, obviously something else is going on here that I'm not aware of."

He shrugged. "I don't want anything to do with Shane. I've asked for a new therapist."

"Wow. Seriously? He's the best that we have. He runs

the entire department. Most people fight to get him."

"Well, no fight from me. Everybody else can have him."

"I presume he said or did something you didn't like."

At that, his head came up, and he gave her a narrow gaze. "Did you talk to him?"

"I said hi to him last night at dinner. He told me that you were struggling with some concepts, but he didn't tell me what it was about."

He searched her face intently for a moment and then relaxed. "I'm glad he didn't. I would consider that a breach of confidentiality."

"I have no intention of getting into personal issues with you, medical or otherwise," she said. "I was just worried. But I gather that you don't want to talk or have anything to do with anybody." She took several steps backward. "If you decide to come down for breakfast, I'll be there." And she turned and walked away.

She bit her bottom lip, wondering what was going on. And what she should do about it, if anything.

XAVIER STARED AT his door after Talia left him, and, for the first time in the last twelve or sixteen hours, he felt like a heel. She wasn't the basis of his ire. Shane was. Xavier didn't have any reason to snap at her. He grabbed his phone and sent her a quick text message saying, **Sorry.** When he got no immediate response, he felt even worse. Didn't mean that she hadn't seen his text, didn't mean that she wasn't sitting there eating and didn't want to respond.

Her failure to respond didn't mean anything, but, of course, in his mind, it was the worst of the worst that he could have done because she'd been nothing but nice to him. More than that, she'd been real, and she'd been honest, and he really liked her. And here he was, acting like a two-year-old and hurting his chances of getting the improvements that he was looking for. When another knock came on his door, Xavier hoped it was Talia. He called out, "Come in." Instead it was Dani.

Dani walked in and said, "Hey, I understand you're having a problem with Shane."

He just stared at her and wasn't sure what to say.

She raised an eyebrow. "Yes or no?" Her tone was clipped, as if this was something that she dealt with all the time.

"I gather you've had a complaint or two against him before."

"Shane? No. Never. He's the best one we have. But, if you won't cooperate and work with him," Dani explained, "then we'll give you to somebody else."

"What do you mean, if *I'm* not cooperative and not working with him?"

She turned and looked at him, her tablet out in front of her. "Not everybody is here to be your friend," she began, "Yet all of us are here to show you where there is room for improvement and what you need to do, including Shane. You don't have to do them. Absolutely you do *not* have to work on the areas that he points out. But you can't expect him to ignore his expertise and to not try to *at least* show you that there is an area for improvement."

He stared at her and swallowed hard. "Meaning?"

She replied, "We all have jobs to do here. That is part of Shane's."

"I suppose he told you all about it," he declared, with a

level of bitterness that surprised him.

"No. You were the one who requested a transfer."

He nodded. "I did. I just thought maybe I would do better with somebody else."

"If you want. Yet Shane works on your specialty, so whatever. If you don't want to have somebody who will get you back on your feet and is doing everything that you stated you wanted to do, that's fine." She clicked away on her tablet. "Mandy has room for another patient."

"Mandy? Who's that?"

"She's one of our newer hires, comes highly recommended though," Dani said. "You'll probably do just fine with her."

"Why?"

"Because she hasn't been here long enough to understand the games the patients play, even with themselves," she murmured. "I've just arranged for the transfer. I'll fill her in right now. You can expect to see her later today." And, with that, Dani was gone.

Leaving Xavier with a sinking feeling that he'd just made a monumental mistake. And one he had no idea how to fix. "No, no, no," he muttered to himself.

Almost immediately he heard footsteps coming down the hallway, and he knew with a sinking heart it would be his new therapist.

She opened the door and, with a bright, cheerful look, stepped inside and greeted him. "Hey, Dani just told me that you're joining my team now. That's perfect. I'm all about teamwork."

And he hated her already. He groaned and asked, "What did Dani tell you?"

"Nothing." She frowned. "Why? Is there a problem?"

"Yeah, there's a problem. I need to be with Shane. Nothing against you."

"Well, it can't be against me," she noted, "because you don't even know who I am. But I can do just as good a job as Shane." She looked down at his chart and then shrugged. "Well, maybe not. Shane is definitely the one who specializes in your kind of injuries, but I'm sure Shane would consult for us."

"Which doesn't make any sense if I'm leaving Shane," he replied.

"And why would you be leaving Shane?" she asked curiously. "He's really good at what he does."

"Apparently," Xavier muttered, staring out the window. "I need to think about this."

"You don't have time," she stated. "We'll have our first session now, so let's get down to the gym and get started on your rehab work."

He glared at her. "No, that won't work out so well for me today."

She stopped in her tracks and frowned at him. "What?"

"I'm not feeling well," he said instantly, grasping at straws to get out of this session.

She hesitated. "I'm not so sure about what to do about that." She checked her schedule on her tablet and suggested, "I have an opening for you tomorrow morning. You think you'll be okay by then?"

"Sure. I'm certain I will be."

She tossed him a bright, sunny smile and said, "Perfect, we'll see you tomorrow morning then at nine." And she turned and walked out.

He crashed back on his bed, realizing that this was not what he wanted at all. But how was he supposed to fix this?

Chapter 9

T ALIA SAW THE text from Xavier and the apology, but Talia wasn't sure what to make of it.

When she glanced over at Shane, who was sitting at her table, having lunch, she asked, "What's going on?"

"He's asked for another therapist," he replied, with a shrug. "Doesn't like what I had to say."

At that, she frowned. "That doesn't sound like him."

"When you touch a nerve," Shane explained, "you can't always tell which way they'll go."

"So who's he got then?"

"Mandy, the new therapist who just came on board."

"Oh," she replied softly.

He looked over at her and grinned. "Yeah. He'll eat her alive."

"Maybe not," Talia replied hesitantly. "But his rehab is the stuff that you specialize in, isn't it?"

He nodded. "Xavier knew that when he made his decision."

"And what if he wants to *un-make* that choice?"

"Then I have to agree to take him back. My schedule's already pretty full. I don't need anybody who's not prepared to step up and do the job." And, with that, Shane gave her a wave and took off, heading back to work.

She sat here for the longest time, wondering how this

was supposed to get fixed. Or maybe it was a good thing, and maybe Xavier would do better with the new therapist. But instinctively she knew there was no way. He was cutting off his nose to spite his face, or whatever that saying was. He had the best physical therapist that he could possibly have for his injuries right here, and Shane had been available. Instead of making the best use of it, Xavier was literally choosing to go with someone who had much less experience and *no* expertise to handle Xavier's injuries. After her lunch, she stopped at Dani's office.

She looked up and smiled. "If this is about Xavier, don't."

"Okay," Talia replied, nodding. "Got it." And she headed back to her own desk.

Talia had plenty of work to keep her busy, but it was hard because she kept thinking about Xavier and what was going on. She didn't quite know what was happening, but, hey, she had to believe that these people were doing the best for Xavier. But what if *he* didn't want the best? What if he was sabotaging his own successes? And that brought up a question she hadn't even considered.

She got up and walked to Dani's desk, leaned against the doorjamb, and asked, "What if he's sabotaging his own progress?"

"He is," Dani confirmed, without even looking up. "That's something he has to figure out himself."

"I hadn't realized just how hardcore you guys are."

"Sometimes we have to be," Dani noted, now looking up at her. "Patients do all kinds of things in order to *not* face the reality of a few things that they're holding on to."

"And I guess I'm not allowed to know what that's all about, am I?"

"Nope, can't do that. HIPAA laws and confidentiality and privacy and everything else," she replied, with a gentle smile. "If he tells you, that's a different story."

"Yeah, I'm not sure he's up for even being friendly right now."

"He's confused and upset, and he's made a choice that he's already regretting," Dani declared.

"Can he go back on it?"

"It would take Shane to okay that. Once a patient asks for a transfer, Shane has the option of not taking back that patient."

"I guess that makes sense too."

"Shane has the right to work with patients who he feels will be best suited for his techniques. And, if that's not Xavier, then Xavier gets to deal with the next therapist. They are all good. Some are just better suited to his medical problems."

"Right," Talia muttered, with a heavy sigh.

As she turned to go away, Dani added, "You need to let it go."

"And how do I do that?" she asked. "I feel as if he's making a monumental mistake."

"He is," Dani agreed cheerfully. "Yet again we can't fix it until he acknowledges that he made a mistake."

"Got it. So is that what you guys are doing?"

"Not necessarily, no," Dani said. "He's got choices to make. He's made one, and now he'll have a whole new rehab therapy. It'll be up to him as to whether that's what he wants to continue with, and we'll accept yet one more change, but we'll hold it back, that change, until he's sure. He made a request in an emotional outburst, and that in itself is damaging, not only for him but for the whole team."

"So why did you let him get away with it?"

"Because he needs to understand that his decisions have consequences," Dani explained. "And we must see that he does want the best for himself, and, if that is this new therapist, then that's what he gets."

"And yet he doesn't know who this new therapist is."

"He'll soon find out, and he'll acknowledge, if only to himself, whether it was a good decision or not."

"And yet he's going backward."

"Backward doesn't happen here," Dani stated. "If he goes forward, he'll have to make a deal with Shane, and that deal will have to be one that Shane can live with too, because he doesn't want anybody who'll quit on him. Shane's time is at a premium here, and I don't blame him."

Talia stared at Dani.

Dani gave her a smile. "Xavier's not the first one to pull something like this, and he won't be the last one."

"No, but it feels as if he's made a huge mistake."

"And maybe he has. Maybe he hasn't. It doesn't matter. It's up to him to fix it. Now I need to return to my work. And, Talia, you need to get back to your job too."

THE NEXT FEW days were tough, as Xavier worked with the new therapist. She was too hesitant and too gentle. He couldn't see any progress, but then, as he had already noted, the progress was progress that he hadn't been necessarily willing to make either. Feeling as if he'd done something wrong just made him angry because he felt that way. He didn't know what to do but proceed down the pathway as if this were the best choice ever.

At the same time he also cut everybody else out of his life. He couldn't face Talia because he didn't know how to explain what he'd done. Xavier didn't want to see Shane, so he refused to show up for mealtimes at the designated hours and so either arrived super early or super late. Plus, he spent half his time in bed, not feeling good.

When he got a phone call from Zander, Xavier whispered, "Well, thank God for that."

Zander asked, "Hey, what's the matter?"

"Nothing," Xavier said.

"Oh, no, no, no, no," Zander replied. "This is me, remember? I know all kinds of things you've pulled in your lifetime, and I'm still here for you."

"Great, because I've just pulled another jerk move, and I didn't even realize it, and I've hurt some people I shouldn't have."

"Wow, you haven't been there all that long. What? A month, a month and a half maybe?"

"Yeah," he muttered.

"What about all the progress?" Zander asked. "They fixed up your stomach, and you were doing great."

"Yeah, up until they brought up some hot-button issues," he muttered, not wanting to share exactly what those issues were and upset his friend. "I asked for a new physical therapist."

There was dead silence on the other end. "So, not Shane, the guy that you told me was absolutely fantastic?"

He winced at that. "No, not Shane, even though I said he was absolutely fantastic."

"Well, in that case, I don't want him either," Zander declared. "Maybe I shouldn't even come."

"No, no, no, no, no, no, *come*," he said. "It is a great

place."

"Doesn't sound like it, not if you're already changing therapists."

"It's not his fault," Xavier grumbled, hating the shame in his words. "It was mine. I had … I had a moment."

"We're all allowed moments," Zander noted. "We're in a bad stage of life, and we have bad things on our plate to deal with."

"Yeah, but, when I had a moment, I did something that I can't really reverse," he explained. "And that's causing me no end of stress."

"Wow, I don't even know what to say to that," his friend admitted slowly, cautiously. "Are you sure you can't reverse it?"

"I don't think so."

"But you don't know because you haven't tried, right?"

"Yeah, that would be about right," he admitted.

"And you haven't tried because you don't want to admit you were wrong?"

He stared across the room, ignoring his friend on the other end.

"Ah, so you've done one of those, *huh*?"

"Yeah, apparently," Xavier conceded, "and you're right. I don't know how to fix it."

"Well, maybe you'll be fine where you are, and maybe this new therapist is great."

"She is great, but she's just not for me," he muttered.

"I'm sorry, man."

"Me too, me too. If you don't mind, I'll get off right now."

"Yeah, sure. If you want to talk later, give me a shout back."

"Yeah, okay, I will, but not for a few days, all right?"

"Yeah, a few days is fine," Zander agreed, "but, if you leave it longer than that, I'll be all over you."

And Xavier knew his friend would.

Just then Zander asked, "Hey, by the way, what was the issue? The hot-button issue?"

"Yeah, I can't talk about that right now. I'll talk to you later." And, with that, he ended the call on Zander too.

Chapter 10

T ALIA WATCHED, TRYING to be friendly, but every turn that she made was rebuffed. Heartbroken, she didn't know what to do. She watched for Xavier over the next few days, but he'd just stepped out of her life.

Dennis came up and whispered to her, "Have you seen him at all?"

She shook her head. "No. He's really struggling with a decision he made, and he won't talk to me about it. He won't talk to anybody, as far as I know," she muttered.

Dennis nodded. "I don't think he's eating," he shared abruptly. "I haven't seen him, and I've been watching for him. I don't think he's coming at odd hours either."

"Have you told Dani?"

"I just did," he said. "I'm not certain what'll happen now."

Talia frowned at that, not sure what the answer would be, but a whole team of medical people were here to help, at least she hoped so. She already knew that she'd pretty well pushed it with Dani in terms of asking questions. Yet, when she looked up later that day, managing to get herself buried in her work, she found Dani standing in front of her, wearing a frown. "Before you ask, no, I haven't talked to him, and he won't talk to me," Talia shared sadly.

Dani nodded. "We'll have to do an intervention then."

"What does that mean?" she asked.

"I've enlisted his psychologist, for one," Dani replied. "Hopefully that will make a difference."

"Do we know what's going on?"

"No, but it all has to do with the same thing. If he's not eating, then that's huge. And I don't know if he is or not, but Dennis is really worried about it."

Talia nodded. "Sometimes people make decisions that they can't live with. And sometimes they think that there is no changing them," she reminded Dani. "So, from their perspective, it's a one-way street. He's probably just waiting to get kicked out of here."

Dani frowned at her. "Why would he even think that way?"

"I don't know, but I wouldn't be at all surprised if he hasn't got something like that going on in his head."

Dani nodded. "Maybe I need to have a talk with him."

"Just be gentle. I think he thinks this is a permanent failure, and everybody's just waiting for him to leave."

"And that couldn't be the furthest thing from the truth," Dani stated, scrubbing her face with both hands. "Sometimes it's not the physical issues that hold people back. It's the emotional ones," she muttered, "and they give us the most trouble."

"I don't think he was trying to cause trouble. I think somebody pushed a button, and he didn't know how to recover."

"Which could be the same thing," she said, with a small smile.

"Maybe, but he's pretty sensitive, so, depending on what was said, that might have been the final word for him."

"Maybe," Dani replied. "I'll think about this. I've got a

shrink on it right now."

"Yeah, let me know if I can do anything to help," Talia offered.

Dani looked back at her. "Is he talking to you at all?"

"No, he isn't," she admitted, "and, yeah, that makes me feel even worse. I feel as if I could have done something, and I didn't."

"Actually you did," Dani declared, facing her. "You tried to talk to me about it."

"Sure, but you have whatever rules or reasons you have for doing stuff," she noted, "and I definitely got the impression that I'm not allowed to get involved."

"Normally it would be a flat-out no for a reply. However, in this case, I'm not sure if that'll work. I'll get back to you." With that, she stepped out.

In a way Talia felt even more confused as to what was happening. The day dragged on, and she just wasn't sure what to do or to say. Now she didn't feel as if she could even go to Xavier's room and talk to him, and that made it even harder. Matter of fact, she didn't have a clue what she had for a choice. It just seemed as if there were no choices, and that was even harder. As she wandered down the hallway, kind of lost, she saw Xavier rolling toward his room, absolute exhaustion on every line of his face. She called out, "Hey, looks as if the new therapy is going really well."

He stared at her for a moment. "Why would you say that?"

Her eyebrows shot up. "Because you look really tired."

"Yeah, well, in that case, it's got nothing to do with the therapist."

"Oh. Sorry." She winced. "I'm not trying to interfere."

He just waved a hand. "It doesn't matter."

"You know people care about what happens to you here, right?"

He looked at her for a long moment. "Maybe. Maybe it's just me." He stared off into the distance. "I made a mistake, and I have some things to work out."

"But no mistake is terminal," she said, trying to get him to see that.

"Most of the time mistakes aren't terminal," he corrected. "Sometimes they are."

She winced. "You're really taking it that hard, *huh?*"

"Yeah, sure am," he declared, staring at her. "Really no other way to take it."

"I think there is," she countered. "I think there's a way for you to go back to whatever it was that you want, without it tearing you apart like this."

He gave her the gentlest of smiles. "Sometimes the things we do are permanent."

"But not always," she argued. "Sometimes we need to acknowledge that mistakes were made, and apologies need to be given, and people just move on," she explained.

He stared at her for a long moment. "Do you really think it's that simple?"

"I do. … No, I've never seen it happen here. I've never seen a scenario like what's going on here right now happen, and, God help me, I hope I never do again," she shared. "I'm really worried about you."

He stopped, his shoulders hunched, and he sighed. "You're probably better if you don't." And, with that, he rolled into his room and closed the door on her.

But now she was starting to get angry. She walked forward, pounded on the door, and opened it. "You don't get to make that decision," she snapped. "Any more than I do. I saw something in you that I really like and that I really appreciate and respect. It's not something I can just turn around and turn off because *you* say so."

An odd look crossed his face as he stared at her. "And what if the people you care about aren't the good people who you think they are inside?"

"No, I refuse to believe that," she murmured. "I can see that maybe confusion, fatigue, emotionalism, all kinds of things, have the ability to hit any of us sideways. And I admit that it's probably fairly traumatizing, but I don't think anything is so bad that it can't be fixed."

"And you could be wrong," he muttered.

"Maybe. Have you eaten today?"

He paused, frowned at her. "Why? You're back to mothering me."

"I *never* mothered you," she declared, recognizing the ploy for what it was, which was to push her away, so he didn't have to deal with more emotions. "I don't know why I care so much, but I do. So I'm here, like a battering ram, reminding you that you still have to eat. You still have to look after yourself."

He stared at her. "Kicking and screaming, whether I like it or not?"

"Absolutely," she snapped. "If I had the physical strength, I would pick you up, stick you in that wheelchair, and drag you down there myself." He stared at her in shock, and she nodded. "There's a time and a place for acting like a two-year-old," she stated. "That time has come and gone. You're hurting yourself physically now.

"I don't know whether you are trying to get yourself kicked out of here or to prove a point that you're some lousy person and everybody should be better off just ditching you, but it doesn't matter because that's not happening. It's not how Hathaway House works. It's not how any of us operate," she announced, loud and proud. "So the sooner you get that worked out of your system, the better." And she turned and walked away.

When she was at the doorway, she looked back at him. "Now I'm going for dinner. I would love it if you would come join me," she murmured. "But if you're still stuck in that self-destructive mode that you were in before, and you're not ready to join the rest of the world, obviously I can't change your mind. However, I'll be in the dining room, if you *do* change your mind."

And she was gone.

THE SWEARING FELL from Xavier's lips, surprising him. It wasn't something he normally did, and most of the time he could control his emotions, but these last few days, this last week? What a nightmare. He'd gone from left to right to left again and seemingly all within the same day, without any rhyme or reason. He had no rudder. He had no control over what was going on, and he hated it.

And yet he knew it was a ship that he had cast offshore of his own making, something that he needed to fix. He just didn't know how or when or even whether it was something he *could* fix. He heard Talia in the back of his head saying, *Of course it is. That's always an option.* And yet he wasn't so sure that she was right.

It seemed as if, more often than not, he just screwed things up when he was on his own. He knew Zander would be very upset with him. But sometimes Xavier just fell into that negative rock pile, and it was almost impossible to get himself back out again. And that felt somewhat where Xavier was at right now. And he didn't know how to fix it.

"Well, she gave you one answer right there. Go down to dinner, try to find some way to be normal, to be grateful that she even offered to eat dinner with you."

And yet he was hot and sweaty and tired, and that was just the beginning of it. And it had nothing to do with his nonphysical workout today. It was all about the emotionalism of his psych session. The psychologist had gotten quite pointed about Xavier's attitude.

Was he up for it? Was he up for meeting Talia in the dining room after having dealt with the psychologist as much as he had, which had been more of a fight than anything? Was he up for making amends? The trouble was, he was lonely. He also felt foolish. She even said he was acting like a child. And he was. He knew that. He just … didn't know how to go forward.

He sat here for a long moment, hating himself, wondering what he was supposed to do, when a knock came on his door. He looked up to see Dani poking her head through. He groaned. "So, are you here to kick me out or to kick me in the butt or what?" he asked.

She looked at him for a long moment. "Which do you need?"

He stared at her, then snorted. "It depends who you talk to. … The shrink? She would probably say I need both. My physical therapist? I'm not even sure she's aware that I have needs that she's not attending to and probably doesn't even know how. And then there's always Talia, who would probably say I definitely needed the kick in the butt but not the *being kicked out* part."

"Why would you think you would get kicked out?" Dani asked curiously. "We work really hard to get a relationship going here with everybody, so I find it interesting when that's the reaction I get."

"Because … I guess I feel as if I don't deserve to be here."

She nodded. "And that's what I would expect."

He looked at her. "I don't get it."

"You're one of a couple who almost automatically think that, as soon as you screw up, you don't get to stay," she shared. "And we do get that sometimes from people, not all of them thankfully, but sometimes. And it's an interesting reaction because, of course, we aren't looking to kick people out of here. We're trying to get you to go through whatever you need to become the best that you can be."

"And when we don't become the best that we can be?" he asked curiously.

She smiled. "I'm not sure that you *aren't* becoming the best that you can be. I'm just not sure that we're giving you the right tools to do it."

"So it's not my fault, it's your fault?" he asked, with a note of humor.

She smiled back. "Oh, I don't know that fault is even involved," she clarified. "Is there definitely some work to be done on your part? Absolutely, but it's up to us to give you the best tools so that you can do it."

He stared at her for a moment. "That's like offering me a cop-out at the same time."

"If that's what you need, maybe that's what you need."

"Talia was just here, telling me that, if I stop acting like a two-year-old, I could go meet her for dinner."

At that, Dani's eyebrows shot up. "That's an interesting

take on it. What was your reaction?"

"Everything from, *I'm too exhausted to deal with it* to *What a good idea.*"

She smiled. "And the exhausted part is something that we always have to remember," she said.

"And yet I don't think Talia was particularly thinking about it."

"No, she's a little more emotional in this area than maybe is good for her."

He nodded. "Meaning, I should just butt out and leave her alone?"

"No, not what I said at all," she declared, looking at him with a knowing smile. "I was thinking more along the lines of maybe not jump down everybody's throats quite so quickly when they offer to do something for you."

"I don't even know why you would bother offering," he murmured.

"I could say it's because that's what we do, but that's not exactly the truth either," she admitted. "In case you haven't figured it out, everybody here is worried about you. Dennis wants me to come drag you down to the dining room and help you eat, even if it means sitting on you and force-feeding you."

Xavier snorted with laughter at that. "Dennis's heart is too big for that body of his, and that's saying something," he muttered.

"It is, indeed. But Dennis knows what happens when you don't give your body enough food to begin to deal with the amount of energy it needs to expend to get through a day of rehab here."

"And I get that too. I wasn't planning on skipping a meal tonight."

"Good, so then did you want to go down and visit with Talia or did you not?"

"I did but …" Dani just waited. He looked at her and asked, "How do you go back on something that you shouldn't have done in the first place?"

"I guess it depends on what you're trying to go back on and what set you off that you felt you needed to go down that pathway in the first place."

"Well, buttons got pushed," he said, with a small quirk of his lips. "It seemed pretty traumatizing at the time, and, of course, now I'm just sitting here wondering what I'm supposed to do."

"Why don't you tell me about it."

He took a deep breath and asked, "You got a minute?"

"Of course I do. Anytime you need to talk to me, just contact me."

He frowned at her and winced. "It's not really in my wheelhouse to do that."

"Then it sounds as if your wheelhouse needs to change," she declared. "People are here to help, whether you think that they're trying to help or not," she said, with a smile.

"Some people are definitely here to help, and others are here to help more than others," he murmured. "And then still more want to help but probably aren't necessarily the right people to help me."

"And that could very well be true," she stated. "Just because we want to help doesn't mean that we're the ones in the position to help."

"So all of that aside," Xavier replied, "I do want to go down. I do want to have dinner with her. I am exhausted. I don't think I can get down there and back. I'm having trouble asking for help while I'm here. It's not something that I thought I would ever have trouble with, but I no longer feel welcome."

At that, Dani let out a slow release of a breath. "Several big issues are right there," she pointed out shrewdly. "Let's deal with the one about whether you're welcome. You're welcome, flat-out, no strings attached. You're welcome. Now have you started something that you're probably not all that happy about? Yes. Does that mean it's something permanent? No. Does that mean it's something that you can change? Yes. Does it mean you want to change? Absolutely not," she declared.

"We all make a lot of choices in life and not just in here. You make choices everywhere all the time. Sometimes we're good with those choices. Sometimes we're not good with them. But it doesn't change the fact that what we have for choices are sometimes regret for the ones that you yourself made. But what we also have is an ability to discuss, to communicate, and to decide on other things in life that are important to you. So, if you want to have dinner with Talia and feel as if you're welcome, I would be the first one to offer to get you down there. But, if you want to do it on your own because you think you can't ask for help or shouldn't ask for help, then that's a problem. *Your* problem."

"What do you mean, you would help me?"

"I would tell you to get your butt in that wheelchair, and I would push you down there. Talia would also very much like to spend some time with you, and she's struggled to stay on her side of this issue and to not interfere and to let you process this on your own," Dani shared. "Also *you* put her in a position that's *not* very easy for her to handle."

"No, of course not," he agreed, with a heavy sigh. "Sometimes I feel like an idiot."

"Or that two-year-old," she pointed out, with a smile.

"Yes, definitely a two-year-old. How is that even possible? I'm well past the age of being a child."

"Because life is a lesson. It's all about dealing with stuff that has to be dealt with. Even if we don't want to, even if we don't think we can, even if it's too hard, even if it's embarrassing. Even if you think you'll lose face, be embarrassed, ashamed, or any other number of very crippling toxic emotions."

"*Toxic*," he muttered. "Yeah, I kinda feel as if I got that part down pat."

She burst out laughing. "Good, that's one thing you figured out then, isn't it?"

"Yeah, but it's not a good thing," he muttered.

"But you have to recognize what you have, what you don't have, and what you're working on," she explained, "and that is something you're expected to do while here."

"Sure, I'm trying, but it's not easy."

She frowned at him. "Easy? Did you find anything *easy* about the last couple years of your life?"

He stared and then slowly shook his head. "No. There hasn't been anything easy about it. I guess when I thought I was doing better that *easy* would be something I could then maybe have in my life. ... It seems as if I have to do everything wrong before I get it right."

"I don't think you're alone in that department," she noted, with a wry smile. "Now, what'll it be? You'll get in that wheelchair and go down and eat?"

"I definitely should. I haven't eaten a whole lot lately."

"We've all noticed. The question is whether you'll do something about it or whether we need to intervene."

"I don't think I want to know what *intervene* means, so I

guess the answer to your question is, yes, I do want to go down there."

"Then get into the wheelchair," she said, pulling it around so that it was right beside him. He looked at her, and she shook her head. "No. When you guys have no problem asking for help, we are always really happy because that makes our job easier. So that wasn't an issue that we expected in your case, and I guess we should have."

"No, I'm just an idiot."

She chuckled. "And again, you don't have a monopoly on that either."

"Meaning?"

"Meaning that a lot of people in this place think that they're idiots. And sometimes we're all idiots. Sometimes you guys say things to us, and it pushes our buttons. We're people too. We have emotions. We have our own things to deal with. We have good days and bad days. Such as, telling me that I'm gonna throw you out, when it is never our policy. Here we are trying our hardest to help you, and you just don't see it."

"Ouch. Okay. Are you trying to tell me that maybe I pushed Shane's buttons too?"

"I'm not telling you anything. Shane is a force unto himself. He handles a lot, but he's also under a lot of pressure."

"I know, and I tend to forget that, don't I?"

"I don't know if you so much forget it, as sometimes it just never even comes into play with people. But Shane has his own very busy schedule, and that can be, in a way, deadly too."

"I guess," he muttered. "Still, I'm sorry."

"Maybe," she murmured. "And that would be good if you are, but I'm not the one who'll fix this."

"Meaning, I have to."

"Yep, because part of what this is all about is life skills, dealing with life."

"I would never have said that I had a problem standing up and saying when I was wrong," he murmured. "So what's wrong with me now?"

Dani smiled. "Nothing, absolutely nothing. But you're no longer in control of your body, and you're no longer in control of what you do on a daily basis, where you can go, or the life ahead of you," she pointed out, "and *that's* the problem."

He stared at her. "Meaning?"

"Meaning that you feel out of control," she replied ever-so-gently. "Yet you are in control. You are the one driving this bus. You are the one making this happen. You are the one working or not working, as you see fit," she murmured. "And, when something unintended blows up, it feels as if you're out of control, as if you're helpless. And you're not," she stated firmly. "If you were a man at a conference or out on a military mission, and you made a mistake, or somebody around you made a mistake, you would expect them to own up to it and to move on, wouldn't you?"

He nodded slowly.

"And that's the stage you're at," she murmured. "You need to own up and to move on."

"And do I still get to stay here?"

"Absolutely," she replied. "But we all know how much *not moving on*, how much making a mistake like that flies in your face, slows your own progress," she noted. "We've all seen it. We all know it can happen, and we all do our darndest to ensure it doesn't happen, trying as much as we can to control that issue. Still it happens. Sometimes things blow up out of control because of stupid little things. However, you are in control of this, and you are not a child, and you can fix this." And, with that, she pushed him forward to the dining room.

Once in line at the buffet, Dennis took one look, and his face beamed. "There he is. What can I get you?"

Xavier checked out the food and felt his appetite starting to build. "I don't know. All of it? I'm starving."

"And that is music to my ears." Dennis prepped him a huge plate. "Now I know this looks like a lot, but you haven't done very well by food lately," he pointed out. "So I can also send you back to your room with a plate because you can't get too much of it in right away."

Xavier stared at it in shock. "I'm not likely to get very much of that at all in my stomach," he murmured.

"You might be surprised," Dennis countered, "particularly if you have some decent company to eat with."

At that, Dani pushed him forward, while he held the tray balanced. When his wheelchair stopped moving, he looked up to see Talia, sitting at a table all alone, staring at him. "Hey, I'm hoping that invitation is still open."

Her smile dawned bright and sweet, and she murmured, "Always. absolutely always."

He felt tears in his eyes that made him feel like a fool.

Talia pushed a chair away that had been beside her and said, "Here, this is a good place for you."

Dani tucked him up next to Talia and announced, "Now, I'll go grab some food for myself." And she turned and left.

Chapter 11

WATCHING DANI PUSH Xavier into the dining room had been both enlivening and also in a way sorrowful because Talia was delighted to see him but obviously he hadn't felt as if he could make it on his own. That he had Dani's help was huge, but that he hadn't asked Talia for help was kind of sad.

She looked over at him. "That's quite a plateful," she said, hoping that was a neutral-enough topic to not upset him.

He nodded. "Dennis even suggested that I might want to take some of it back to my room for later, in case my stomach couldn't handle all of it right now," he murmured, as he stared at it. "I'm not sure I can even begin to eat much of this."

"I wouldn't either, since you've been a little chintzy on the food lately."

"If you mean the fact that I haven't eaten at all, you're right. But I am trying to work on that."

"Good. I'm glad Dani helped you get here. I would have, if I'd known," she said impulsively.

He nodded. "I know you would have. I guess I was feeling … It's my fault. I was struggling with feeling as if I shouldn't even be here. Or I shouldn't be doing what I was doing or I was in the wrong. I don't know," he admitted.

"I've spent so much time at the shrink's today that I don't even know if I'm coming or going."

She pealed with laughter, and it was such a beautiful sound that he had to smile. But it was her heart that was light as a feather at his words.

"No matter what age you are, lessons don't get any easier. We have all these things that we deal with here," she explained. "Sometimes it seems as if we're getting somewhere, and then sometimes it seems as if we're just not getting anywhere," she murmured. "But, in your case, I'm really happy to know that you feel as if maybe something is working."

"I don't know about *working*," he clarified. "I'm still winding my way through all that, but I've got lots to think about, so maybe that's a good thing."

"It's definitely a good thing," she declared, with a smile. "Now, let's see if we can get you to eat some of that food there."

"Well, I'm hoping so," he muttered. "I know Dennis will be back around in a little bit if I don't."

"You got that straight." She chuckled. "But, just in case you think he does it to be a nosy busybody, he doesn't. He does it because he cares and because he worries."

"I get that," Xavier admitted, "and that's something else that's so very strange. I'm only used to having Zander care."

"And, without Zander, you kinda lost your rudder, haven't you?"

He sighed. "And that sounds so stupid."

"Maybe, but I think it's kinda true."

"It is," he agreed. "I just hadn't really thought about it in that way before."

"Sometimes relationships help, and sometimes it's good

to have a break," she murmured.

"And I guess at this point in time, it's been *good to have a break*." And, with that, he picked up a fork and started eating.

"So," she began, trying to resist frowning. "You needed a break from me?" she asked, almost afraid of his answer.

Xavier shook his head. "No. Not at all. Our relationship is the best one I've got. I was referring to Zander."

"A break from Zander?" she repeated.

He nodded. "If you don't mind, I don't want to get into that any further—not right now. Maybe later."

She nodded, happy he had explained that better to her. Yet his words completely surprised her. She hadn't expected him to acknowledge that there was a problem in the relationship with Zander or that Xavier needed to have something in his life that was a little bit separate and distinct from his friend's. Still, it was all good. Xavier was doing so well.

As he chomped his way through the food with an appetite that surprised her, she looked over at Dennis and smiled. He gave her the thumbs-up, and then he went back to looking after other patients.

She smiled at Xavier. "Don't look now, but Dennis is beaming because you're eating."

He smiled at her. "Well, let him beam on, because today I'm starting to feel as if maybe I'll live through this."

"You will," she declared, with a vote of confidence that she truly felt for the first time in a long time. "I'm sure you will. And thank you for sharing what's on your mind with me."

XAVIER SLOWLY FELT better as he ate, even though some foods still made him sick. Still, he knew it was mostly about the thoughts that circled through his mind while he was eating. He knew he would have to do something about that. So he decided he would talk to Mandy, his physical therapist, the next day.

That next morning, he renewed his resolve. "Hey, Mandy, would you be terribly upset if I asked to go back with Shane?"

She stopped and looked at him.

He shrugged. "I feel as if I have done him a disservice. I feel as if I'm doing you one too right now."

She dropped to the floor beside him and sat cross-legged. "Maybe we should talk about that."

"Maybe, but I have some fences to mend with Shane."

"Are you sure that Shane feels there are fences to mend?"

He gave her a lopsided smile. "I'm not sure what Shane would think. I just know that I feel I should."

"In that case, why don't you talk to Shane first?"

"I should. I need to do it, but I've been hesitating."

She studied him for a long moment. "I'm new here. I'm not exactly sure how the system works in this scenario," she began, "but you need to work with whoever you feel can get you the best results."

"I don't want to insult you," he added.

She shook her head. "No, that's not, … not part of this at all. I want you to be honest, and, if I'm doing something that you don't like, then tell me that."

He smiled at her. She was so earnest and serious that he didn't want to upset her at all because she was trying so hard. He shook his head. "No, this is something that happened before you ever got here."

She nodded. "I heard something about it from some-body, but I don't know the details."

"And honestly, the details are just nothing," he noted. "It's … it's my fault. I was stupid. Shane pushed some of my buttons, and I asked for a transfer."

"And now you want to go back to him?"

"I feel as if I hurt the relationship between him and me, and, more than that, it's hurt me," he shared. "I feel as if I need to make things right."

"And does making things right mean you don't want me to be your therapist?"

He studied her for a moment. "Meaning, you think that I should make peace with him and then see how I feel?"

She shrugged. "I won't say that but if, if you can do something to make things better for yourself, then you need to do it." She smiled. "What I don't know is what that'll take."

"I don't either," he murmured. "Of all the things in life that I thought would be easy, or at least simple, it turns out that this was one of the worst."

"Anything emotional or anything we feel we've done wrong and need to make amends for," she noted, "is always traumatic."

He chuckled. "Isn't that the truth? Let me make my most abject apologies to Shane and see where we stand."

"The other thing is," she added, "and I get that you may want to go back to Shane, and, if that's something that can be arranged, absolutely. The other thing is, he'll be working with me on a couple other patients," she shared, "so, if that's something that we can make happen, you can also end up still with me but also with Shane."

"And that might be an easy answer too," he noted. "I

really don't know if Shane even has room to take me back."

She winced. "I know he's incredibly overbooked."

"Of course he is," Xavier muttered, staring off in the distance. "And it would be my fault for having done what I did."

"But these changes aren't permanent," she murmured. "So, go talk to Shane first."

"Right, now all I need is courage."

At that, she rose to her feet. "Maybe the question here is, do you feel as if you did something wrong and you need to go apologize so that *you* feel better, or did you *not* do something wrong and need to apologize because you're still feeling lousy?"

"I definitely didn't do something right," he conceded.

"And, of course, not doing something right is very different from doing something wrong," she pointed out. "Some of us work better together than others, and that doesn't mean that what you did was wrong."

"No, but it wasn't as good as it could have been, … as *I* could have been," he corrected. "And that matters to me."

"Good enough," she replied cheerfully. "Then go figure that out, and let me know what's happening."

"I will. Thank you."

As she walked out, he looked to see if she was upset, but there was no sign of it in her stride, but that didn't mean a whole lot. This really was a problem from before she arrived. So it was a hard thing for him to explain away. It was definitely something that he had to deal with in his own time, but he was also out of time. Mandy was good at what she did. Xavier just didn't feel as if she was good enough for what he needed. And that just made him feel worse because, of course, he'd already walked away once from a physical therapist. Now here he would do it again.

And he didn't know what the options were at this point in time, but he needed to do something in order to at least heal the rift that he felt he'd caused. He rolled his way down to Shane's desk, but he wasn't there. Xavier looked around but saw no sign of him. Nothing. He found a notepad and wrote down a quick message, saying he would like to see him. And then he thought about it and realized that maybe he was still on the fence. He crumpled up the note.

With that, he headed back to his room to see if Shane's contact info was on his tablet. And sure enough it was there. Yet he wondered at just what point in time Xavier would get taken off this contact information sheet that he was utilizing. … The whole thing made him feel weird. But, hey, he had a lot to learn. He sent Shane a message on the tablet regardless.

Xavier was tired, emotionally overwrought, and nothing like knowing you had an apology to make to have you feeling as if the rest of your day would be downhill. As it was, he didn't hear from Shane all that afternoon. He frowned at that and wondered whether he was supposed to do something else in order to get a chance to talk to him or Shane was just now not even part of his world because Xavier had made it that way. Did Shane not communicate with anybody other than his assigned patients? It felt stupid, and it felt weird, but Xavier didn't know what to do.

Finally he went down to dinner to find Shane sitting at a table with several other staffers, obviously deep in a meeting of some kind. And Xavier couldn't blame the guy, depending on what was going on with the patients here. That meeting could be even about Xavier.

At that thought, he winced and quickly rolled over to

Dennis and asked, "Hey, you got something easy on the stomach?"

"Another bad day?"

"Nerves," he said, shooting a glance to where Shane was.

"He doesn't bite, you know?"

Xavier eyed Dennis and then flushed a deep dark red. "Does everybody know?"

"Nope," he replied. "I'm just a little more intuitive than a lot of people."

At that, he stared at Dennis and nodded. "I can certainly agree with that. You are, indeed. I'm not sure whether that's a good thing or not though."

"Neither do I," Dennis said. "Sometimes I feel as if I see something going on around me, and I can't fix it because nobody else is really there ready to fix it. And then, when they are ready, it's hard to get a hold of people."

"Because it depends on other people's time too," Xavier muttered. "Right, and that would imply that I hurt them."

"I don't know about *hurt*," Dennis clarified, "but there are also professional qualms about working with people again. All kinds of issues come up with each situation." He added, "But I can tell you that it isn't the first time, and, given the work he does and the people that he has to deal with, it won't be the last time."

Xavier stared at Dennis. "I don't think I feel any better."

Dennis burst out laughing. "I'm not sure I intended to make you feel better," he admitted, with a smile. "The thing is, this is life. When something happens, you fix it."

"Got it. I've sent him a couple messages, so I guess he'll talk to me when he gets time," Xavier said.

As far as dinner, he stared at the food and nothing, nothing appealed. "Maybe I'll just skip dinner tonight." He turned and rolled away, leaving Dennis standing there, open-mouthed.

Dennis came racing behind. "I would just as soon you didn't skip dinner," he said.

"Maybe, but my stomach's already talking back at me, and I don't want to go through another food-down, food-up scenario," he muttered. "So maybe I'll just wait."

And, with that, ignoring Dennis but hating to see the look of distress on his face, Xavier slowly moved toward his room. All he could hope for was that maybe his stomach would calm down, and maybe he could eat a little bit later. But, if it didn't calm down, there was absolutely no point in eating because it would just be a brutal night. And that he didn't need.

Chapter 12

TALIA WALKED INTO the dining room to see Xavier rolling back toward his room. She looked over at Dennis and frowned. He motioned for her to come over. "What's going on?" she asked him.

"Aah, he's chosen not to eat tonight," he shared in a low tone. "Says his stomach's pretty rough, and he's waiting for Shane. He sent Shane a couple messages."

"Ah, so it's nerves."

Dennis nodded. "I think he's feeling pretty badly."

"I think he is too." She turned and stared back toward the general location of his room. "I would take him something, but, if it is nerves, he won't eat it, or it will come back up, and that's the last thing we want."

Dennis nodded. "Shane has also been in a meeting most of the afternoon, so he won't get to Xavier anytime soon."

"Not to mention the fact that Shane is also trying to have a life and to find some peace and quiet in his world."

"Yep, I hear you," Dennis replied. "But, in this instance, maybe we can convince Shane that he needs to spend a few minutes with Xavier first."

She nodded. "But Shane has to be free and clear for that."

Almost as if they heard their comment, the staff meeting seemed to break up, and everybody stood and split off into groups.

She looked over at Dennis. "Are they not coming here for dinner?"

He shrugged. "I suspect a bunch will, but a lot probably want to go back to their desks first."

And, with that, Dennis stood ready at the buffet counter to help people who came by looking for food. She spotted Shane, but he was slowly leaving the dining room, while talking with some of the people who were in the meeting.

Talia separated him with a quick call out.

He gave her a quick frown and asked, "Do I need to handle this right now? I'm trying to get out of here."

"I know." She took a deep breath. "And I get that you're swamped and that you're busy."

He shook his head. "And this isn't about you, so what's going on?"

She quickly explained that Xavier had sent him two messages and had been in to get food and then had wheeled away because he didn't think he could handle anything.

"And I thought he was doing much better," Shane replied, frowning.

"Yes, he was, but he's determined to talk to you, and *not* talking to you is making him sick." At that, Shane's eyebrows shot up. She nodded. "Yes, as in sick to the stomach with stress and with nerves."

"Jesus." Shane looked at his watch, frowned, started to shake his head as if to say he wouldn't make it, and then muttered, "Fine. Let me see if I can talk to him." And, with that, he bolted off toward Xavier's room.

She looked back over at Dennis, but he had a big smile on his face. He gave her a thumbs-up. The trouble was, she wasn't sure whether she'd done anything good or not. At this point in time the men had to work it out themselves. But as much as it appeared to be a big deal for Xavier, she wasn't so sure how big a deal it was for Shane. He dealt with people like this all the time. He dealt with scenarios like this all the time, although maybe not quite like this. But it's obvious that he didn't want Xavier to suffer any more than he was. And that was a good thing. Because Xavier was suffering, and she didn't want to see him go downhill any faster than he already was. And that was a problem too.

XAVIER WAS IN bed, pulling the blanket up over him, an arm over his head. He really didn't feel well. He didn't know if he was having a relapse or whether it was just stress, but, whatever it was, it was not good. His insides kept cramping, and his whole body shook. He slowly worked on his breathing, trying to calm it down, even though he had no reason for it to be stressed. And to think that this was knocking him out as badly as it was didn't say anything good.

When a knock came on his door, he muttered, "If you have to come in, come in."

"That's not a very nice welcome," Shane replied. He stepped in, took one look at Xavier, and asked, "Good Lord, what's wrong?"

Xavier opened his eyes and muttered, "I don't know, but my stomach is cramping. I figured it was just stress."

"If so, you are giving yourself an ulcer."

"That wouldn't be good. I don't know what it is. But my back doesn't feel good, and my gut doesn't feel good either."

At that mention of his back, Shane stepped forward and

took a closer look. "What's going on with your back? Can you sit up so I can take a look?"

Slowly, with Shane's help, Xavier sat up, feeling his back *ping* with pain.

"What exercises are you doing?"

He went over the exercises that he was working with Mandy on.

Shane said, "I'll talk to her."

"About what?" Xavier asked.

"Some of these need to be shifted out," he murmured. "Your back's not handling these. They are causing more stress on your system."

"We've hardly been working," Xavier noted. "It seems she's a much lighter touch than you."

"That's what you wanted, wasn't it?"

"Hell no, and you know it," he said.

Shane studied him. "I hear you left me some messages.'

"Yeah, I did." And then he felt like an idiot. "I'm sorry."

At that, Shane picked up the tablet, then asked him, "Sorry for what?"

"For being a jerk."

The corner of Shane's mouth kicked up. "You really haven't cornered the market on being a jerk in this place."

Xavier cracked a small smile. "I guess not, *huh*?"

"A lot of people come through here with scenarios similar to yours, and we've been through it time and time again. Still, everyone is different. Every case is different. And your case is just an interesting side note of something even more different."

"That doesn't sound good."

"It's not meant to sound bad either," Shane noted. "Part of the problem with you is, you don't want anybody pushing your buttons."

"No, I did not want anybody pushing my buttons," he admitted, "but it doesn't seem as if anybody'll listen."

At that, Shane burst out laughing. "Very true. We're here to help you heal. We're not here to make life look pretty and flawless."

"I hadn't really seen that rehab with Mandy was that much of a difference for a while," Xavier shared. "And now honestly, a lot of my life is just in the toilet."

"That is not good. Stretch out and roll over."

Xavier snorted. "You make it sound as if I can just do that."

"Well, you *were* doing that."

"But I haven't done that in a while."

Tight-lipped, Shane assisted him in a rollover. "I'll work on your back here for a minute to see what's going on." Several painful minutes later, he added, "And, of course, you've been pushing it."

"Pushing what?" He grunted as Shane poked a spot that hurt.

"Looks as if you've got a pinched nerve here. I just can't understand why you haven't been screaming in pain."

"I have been, but there's pain, and then there's pain."

At that, Shane glared at him and dropped into the chair beside him. "So what is it you want to do?"

"I want to go back to having you as my physical therapist," he replied instantly. "If you'll take me back."

"Ah, that's what's causing all this stress, isn't it?"

"Everybody made it very clear that you were under no obligation to take me back. And I was certainly aware of how badly I'd behaved and how overbooked you are and that there was a good chance you wouldn't want anything to do with me. So, yeah, I made a mistake, and it felt major as soon as I made it, with no way to fix it."

"You didn't behave badly at all," Shane replied. "It's important for you to express emotions and to make decisions for yourself. And you did that. You made a decision, and you expressed how you felt about it, and that's just life."

"And what if I want to change that decision?" he asked.

"I am really swamped," Shane replied, a frown on his face.

"So swamped that I can't come back on board?"

"It's not just about PT sessions, but I'm taking on some new duties here, which are also taking up a ton of my time," he muttered.

Xavier suggested, "The other option would be that you work with my current therapist and have her do the specifics that you tell her to do."

"The trouble with that is, Mandy doesn't know these exercises. She doesn't have the training."

"So then I go to her for what? Balance and flexibility, and I go to you for more."

"And that would double up on your PT sessions," Shane noted, "but, as I can see, you've already slipped backward."

At that, Xavier froze. "Badly?"

"Badly," Shane declared in disgust. "It'll take us another week or two to get you back up to par. You can't afford setbacks like this."

And he knew that Shane was speaking more out of frustration than anything, but it sounded bad. "Right," Xavier muttered, "so I messed up even more than I thought."

Shane sighed. "First off, you didn't mess up. Second off, it's what happens when you don't continue on a specific program. I left notes in the file, but I should have double-checked what she was doing is what needed to be done. Honestly, the time's just gotten away from me."

"I haven't exactly been a part of your radar."

"No, I got several more patients at the same time that you switched out, so I've got a lot of work right now."

"Sounds as if Hathaway needs to hire more people."

"If we could find the right people, we would," he murmured. "It's not that easy. Some of these skills are very specialized," he explained. "I've been contacting people who went to some of the last training sessions who seemed really capable, to see if they wanted a job. I'm hoping I can convince a couple of them to come in this next week or so."

"Anyone in particular?" he asked, frowning.

"Sure, Eve's one of them. She's pretty dynamic, but I also know that she's in high demand, so I also have to see if I can find others. There were a couple others. Eve's got a twin sister, Yvette, and she might end up coming, but it depends whether her husband will move because they're not local."

"Right. I didn't even think about that."

"Staffing's always an issue," Shane noted. "The work we do is very important, and it's not always something that we can just hand off," he said, with a side glance over at Xavier.

"Got it. Too bad I didn't realize that in time."

"You've realized it in time for you. However, it's just not the easiest timing for me. Look. I'll make it work," he muttered. "I'm not sure how yet. We'll get you back on the roster, but I have three conditions."

At that, Xavier stared at him, mute. "Go ahead. What are they?"

Shane raised one eyebrow. "What? You're not jumping in and saying *absolutely?*"

"No, not until I've heard them," Xavier said.

"Good, at least then you'll think about them. One, this is the only time we do *take-backs*," he stated, using a childhood term that made them both smile. "Two, you'll have to work harder to regain what you've lost. … I'm not happy, not at all."

"And I get that. So I don't have a problem with that. Yet it's a little more maybe than I thought it was, in the sense that I'm even struggling to get food down."

"And part of that is because you're not getting the bowels moving," he pointed out. "It's hard to continue on this pathway when you're in pain. That brings me to my third requirement. The fact is, you've been *lying* about the pain, and that's gotta stop."

He stared at Shane. "You figured that out, *huh?*"

"Yeah, I figured that out," he snapped, "and no more. We can't progress if we can't get pain managed, and then all the work to be done will hurt you, so you can't progress. Thus it all comes back to pain management."

"Right," he muttered. "So the answer is yes, yes, and yes."

"Good. I'll make it happen. However, I don't know that I can make it happen tomorrow."

"I don't also want to hurt her feelings."

He looked over at him. "You mean Mandy?" He nodded. "I wouldn't worry about it. Just like everything else in life, it's a learning curve. And, if you've already spoken to her about it, which you probably have—"

"I did, and she was okay with it. I just feel as if maybe she's not okay with it."

"I'll talk to her," Shane repeated. "In this industry we have patients move all the time. I'm just a little busier than some of them."

"No, not some of them," Xavier corrected with a smile. "You're just crazy busy."

"I am. My time has become a huge issue here."

"Well, I'm grateful," he muttered. "Please know that."

"I know. Now, you need to get your butt back down to the kitchen and get some food down."

He shuddered. "I'm not sure I can."

At that, Shane frowned. "If you can't, it'll be hard to get any work done with you."

"Fine, I'll go see what I can get down."

"Don't make it too heavy, don't make it too large, but get some nutrients—at least a soup, salad, some protein." Shane added, "Without the protein, your muscles cannot rebuild."

"I know. You told me about that."

"Great, too bad you didn't listen." And, with a big grin on his face, Shane walked out, leaving a much-relieved Xavier in his wake.

Chapter 13

TALIA SAT AT a table in the dining room, working on her meal, her stomach knotting at the thought of whatever Xavier was going through right now. Did she dare go see him after dinner or should she wait until tomorrow morning?

Dennis came up behind her and whispered, "Don't look now."

She instinctively turned to see Xavier, rolling his way slowly into the dining room.

Dennis walked toward him and asked, "Hey, you feeling better?"

"A little bit," he said. "I need to get some food down. Shane says otherwise I won't get any of the needed work done tomorrow."

"That's good news," Dennis replied.

"He's at least talking to me," Xavier shared, with a smile. "But now I don't … I don't know what I can get down. Honestly, my stomach's still pretty rough."

"In that case, let's go back to the basics," Dennis suggested. "How about just a baked potato with some butter?"

Xavier considered it and nodded. "Except he told me to get some protein for the muscle building."

"How about a shake?" Dennis offered instead. "Sometimes, despite our best efforts, we can't get food down at certain times."

WHEN HE FINALLY made a couple choices, he looked around and frowned. "Is everybody already done?"

"Mostly, but you may want to head over there."

And then he saw Talia, still eating.

"Sure, that would be nice."

"And I'll bring your meal over to you in just a minute."

Xavier slowly made his way over to Talia and asked in a quiet voice, "May I sit here?"

She smiled at him in delight. "Absolutely." He rolled up beside her and sat in place. "No food?" she asked.

"Dennis is bringing it," he murmured. "I guess I look like the cat dragged me into a mud puddle."

"Oh, you do, but everybody around here is used to seeing that, or going through it themselves."

He smiled, for the first time feeling a sense of relief and realizing how much these people came from heart. "I'm hoping I'm over the worst of it."

"It depends what the worst of it is," she noted.

"Shane's willing to take me back."

She stared at him in joy.

Yet Xavier shrugged. "The thing is, he wants me to eat in order to build muscle. He's not very happy with what I've lost since changing therapists, so I definitely set myself back."

"And that could just as easily have been your emotional stuff taking its toll too."

"Yeah, apparently that has to be over with now too," he shared, with a smile.

"And hopefully it will be," she said. "It's easy for people to say what should be done, but we all know that sometimes things take longer to get over."

"Well, I'm definitely prepared to get back to work with him tomorrow. He'll also talk to Mandy."

"And I suppose you're also worrying yourself sick about her."

"Well, sure. I feel as if I screwed over a bunch of people."

"You screwed nobody over," she stated firmly. "This is the job, all part of rehab of the mind, body, and soul."

Xavier stared at her, but, before he could respond, Dennis arrived with a large baked potato and a piece of steak.

"If you can't eat all the steak, that's fine. If you want some greens, that's fine too."

"He did tell me to get lots of vegetables down but no way I can handle all this tonight."

"How about a green shake to help you out?"

"Sure. I might manage that, even if I have to finish it in my room. It might be the only thing I manage," he said, pointing at his meal. "I really hate it when food goes to waste."

"So take your time, sit here, relax, de-stress," Dennis suggested, with a hard look at him. "And you'll be surprised what appeals." And, once again after imparting words of wisdom, Dennis walked away.

Xavier looked over at Talia and smiled. "It continuously surprises me how much everybody cares here."

"So you've mentioned a few times," she said cheerfully. "When one thing goes wrong, it affects everybody."

He nodded. "And I'm sorry for my part in that," he murmured.

"And you need to stop being sorry," she replied, giving him a direct look. "Because, just like for everybody else, it's life. We make decisions. We make changes. We do the best we can. Then we learn, we pick up, and we move on."

He smiled. "Well, consider me to have been picked up and now moving on."

She laughed. "I'll believe that when I see you eat. We all know how bad it is when you don't."

"Hey, I'm eating." He picked up his fork and dug into the potato. "I'm eating."

Chapter 14

T ALIA WAITED IN the dining room the next morning to see Xavier. When there was no sign of him at breakfast time, she got worried. She sent him a quick text and asked if he was okay. He sent back a thumbs-up but nothing else. She wasn't exactly sure what that was all about, but, after last night, she could only hope that maybe Shane had squeezed in Xavier first thing this morning. She really wanted to talk to Shane but also knew that she needed to stay out of it.

Sometimes being caring was good, and other times it really wouldn't help anybody. Also she could easily be perceived as interfering, and that wasn't where she wanted to go with this. She had to trust Xavier.

She smiled as she thought about that because that's exactly what this was all about. *Trust.* Xavier would fill her in whenever he could. She could trust Xavier that he cared enough to tell her what was going on. She also believed him to be perfectly capable of making this happen. Whatever it was that he needed to make happen, he could do it. She knew that. This guy was magical in so many ways. He just had to believe a little bit more in himself.

And she was nobody to criticize that because she understood. Life in just so many ways could mess you up, and weren't we all living proof in so many ways? So she moved through her day, waiting for any word from him. Her workday got super busy around lunch, so she ended up late to the dining room. By the time she got there, the crowd had already dispersed.

Dennis smiled at her. "Hey, I wondered if you would make it."

"The more I tried to get here," she shared, "the more things were blowing up."

"I get that," Dennis noted. "It's good that you made it at all."

"Some days, just even getting here is the accomplishment of the day," she stated, with a laugh. She looked around. "And everybody's gone already, haven't they?"

"Yep, you missed it."

"What did I miss?"

"I don't know exactly. Everybody came, and Xavier was with a group of people, including the therapist. They seemed to be having some heavy talks."

She nodded slowly. "Okay."

"And other than that, I have no idea."

"Did you get any update?" she asked Dennis.

"We'll find out when he's good and ready," Dennis replied.

And she agreed, but waiting was difficult. She grabbed a quick lunch and headed back to her office. When she lifted her head hours later, Dani was quietly staring at her. "What?" Talia asked, putting down her pen and rubbing her eyes.

"You're working hard."

"Believe it or not, Dani," she teased, "I always work hard."

"I know, and it's hard sometimes when you are affected by what's going on."

"Do we have a solution to what's going on though? That's the real issue."

"I think so," Dani replied cheerfully. "I think they're working it out."

"That would be nice, but it would also be nice if somebody filled me in on it."

At that, Dani laughed. "No can do, but I'm sure he will soon."

She nodded. "I'm trusting in that. And that's what it's all about, isn't it?"

Dani nodded. "Trust is huge," she admitted. "And it's not just being told what's going on but being let into the inner circle so that you can understand the nuances of how it all went down."

"Xavier did tell me that Shane was taking him back, but his progress had slid in the interim."

"Again, that's okay too."

Talia waited to hear more throughout the rest of the day. When it came time to call it quits at work, she still hadn't heard from him. As she got up and shut down her computer, Shane popped in.

"Hey. Oh, you just shut off your computers."

"Yeah, what do you need?"

He said, "I was looking for some more information on this one patient file. My computer just keeps crashing."

She groaned at that. "We need more IT staff in here."

"Or you guys need to stop messing with the system," Dani called out.

Shane grinned at that. "That might help too. But Talia's right, more in-house IT people would be helpful."

"Yeah," Dani added, joining them at the doorway, "but do we need a full-time IT person, just to be here on the off-chance that we run into a glitch? They are kinda high-end personnel."

"Don't you have a former patient who's computer savvy or something?" Talia asked. "Somebody who would be happy to come back to work and just work as a full-time IT?"

"We've tried a couple IT personnel in the past," Shane noted. "They were part-time hires back then. That didn't work out so well."

Dani looked over at Talia and shared, "Maybe once I get through the next budget meeting, I'll try to figure out something. The worklist for IT is never-ending."

"It is here, especially because of patient records, and the volume of things that we send back and forth."

Dani nodded. "I know. Let me think about it."

"Yvonne. What about Yvonne Britman?" Shane asked.

Dani frowned at him. "What about her?"

"She just moved back to town. She's in IT. She would love a chance to work here. She was also interested in attending one of the adaptation rehab programs that I'm putting together, for those who have already been through the program."

"Why would she come back to rehab?" Dani asked.

"Because she had a car accident," Shane shared. Dani gasped. "I know, right? As if that poor woman hasn't had enough."

"Was she driving?" Dani asked.

"No, and, not only that, she was hit by a car in a pedestrian crosswalk. So she's been through some therapy, and she's had a lot of work done. Overall she's doing really well, but she knows that she now needs to tweak some of the exercises that she had been doing that just aren't quite right to handle this latest injury."

"So are you are doing some personal PT work with her?" Dani asked.

"I suggested she sign up for the weekend workshops," Shane replied. "We just need more people to sign up to justify running them."

"Right," Dani agreed. "Do you have a contact number for her?" she asked him.

"Yeah, I do," Shane searched his tablet and found her number and handed it over.

"Who is this Yvonne woman?" Talia asked.

"She was a patient here for a long time," Shane explained, with a smile. "She and Dennis really hit it off, but it obviously wasn't the right timing for them. However, she's back in Dallas now, and she's dealing with a whole new set of problems."

"Well, that can be really tough in itself," Talia murmured. "I mean, it's one thing to go through everything that she probably went through already and another thing entirely to sit here and figure out how to make all her old injuries now sit up and work with the new injuries."

"Thankfully she's not that badly injured," he said. "Still, it was a huge setback for her. She'd been doing so well too."

And before Talia realized it, Dani was already on the phone, calling Yvonne.

Shane looked over at Talia. "That's Dani for you. Give her an inch, and that girl will take a running mile."

"Don't have much choice, with you guys around here," Dani noted, holding a hand over the speaker on her cell phone. With a wave to them, Dani returned to her own office.

Meanwhile, Talia returned to Shane's request. "Fingers

crossed that my computer is glitch-free." She found what Shane was looking for and printed him a hard copy. "Now, get lost."

With a big grin, he did just that.

It left her sitting alone in her office, as she thought about what she wanted to do next. She really wanted to talk to Xavier but wanted to give him some space too. And yet her phone buzzed around the same time with a text from him. She smiled as she read it, then sent back a text. **Hey. How're you doing?**

He sent her a happy face.

How about coffee on the deck? she asked.

Immediately his answer came back. **Too hot.** Then he phoned her. "I'm down at Stan's," he greeted her, his voice soft. "I'm cuddling a bunch of kittens."

"I'll be there in a minute." Talia pocketed her phone and headed to the veterinary. She loved being with the animals and yet didn't spend anywhere near enough time here. As she walked in, Robin was on duty.

Robin smiled at Talia. "Hey, so I heard Xavier call you and tell you to get your butt down here."

"I think about coming down here all the time, but life's just been so crazy busy upstairs," Talia explained. "It seems as if it's been weeks since I've even had a chance to visit."

"Oh, I get it," Robin agreed. "We're in the same boat here. Days can go by, and everything's fine, and then the next thing you know, it just all blows up, and you're scrambling to stay above water."

"For you too, *huh*?"

"Oh, yeah," she said, with a sigh. "Even though we try hard to keep sanity in place, it doesn't always work." Robin waved Talia to come join her.

So she came around the front counter, where one of the women was on the phone. Talia smiled and gave her a thumbs-up and followed Robin into the back. There, Talia found Xavier sitting on a chair, with a great big armful of kittens.

Robin hung around, watching the kittens too.

Talia stared at him and the beautiful kittens. "Good Lord, how precious."

He beamed at her. "I needed some animal influence."

"Ya think?" she teased. "I'm kinda jealous."

"You can take a couple, but you can't disturb them."

She snickered. "So how am I supposed to take a couple and not disturb them?" She did try, but it just didn't work out so well. Finally she just sat down beside Xavier with one kitten in her arms. The little one looked up at her trustingly and made a tiny little blip with his tongue and then curled up against her chest. She sighed happily. "What is it about that wonderful trust an animal gives you," she shared, "that just makes you feel on top of the world?"

It was Robin who answered. "That's what it is. It's trust. It's that innocence of Mother Nature who believes in you, believes in what you can do for her. And that you'll be there to hold her, even when she falls asleep." Which, as they looked down on the kitten in Talia's arms, appeared to be completely out.

"They're really beautiful," Talia murmured. "Didn't you have kittens the last time I was here?"

"Puppies, kittens, we always have pretty well some of each," Robin replied, with a smile. "And thankfully the girls at the front desk handle a lot of the adoptions, so we can move some of them to good, healthy homes."

"Some?" Talia repeated.

"Actually we do really well placing them. Plus, we work with a couple rescues in town. So, when those rescues come through our clinic, we have to give the animals the full once-over, wellness checks, usually spaying or neutering as required," Robin explained. "Often they have eye infections and just general respiratory issues. Things can come, and things can go, but almost always a couple rescues will need something."

"And do you do that free of charge?" Talia asked.

"Yes," Robin shared, "and, before you ask, there's never enough donation money."

Talia looked over at Xavier, who was nodding, as if that confirmed something in his head. She just smiled at him.

Xavier said, "A need is everywhere, isn't there?"

"Isn't that the truth," Robin murmured. "It's sad in a way, but, in another, it's just the cycle of life. We do what we can with who and with what we can."

"I guess donations come your way in dribs and drabs," Talia noted.

"And we're blessed to have a bunch of people who donate on a regular basis. Dani's always really good at getting donors, but Stan donates much of his time. I tend to donate a lot of my time. At some point, you wonder if it'll ever slow down. The answer is, it really won't. This is what we have to deal with. Lots of it is good, lots of it is rough. But we do the best we can to give everybody a fair shot. ... And these guys need to go into the back and get their food."

"Is it feeding time?" he asked.

"It is, indeed. I've been waiting Stan to get clear of the one room that I prefer to take them into. If you guys have five minutes and can hold a couple each," she said, "I'll take a couple to bottle-feed them."

"Or," Xavier suggested hopefully, "you could bring us a couple bottles each, and we could give you a hand."

Robin nodded. "I won't say no to that offer." And she disappeared.

XAVIER SMILED WHEN Robin handed him two bottles. He relinquished two kittens to Robin, plus one more to Talia, so that he now held two kittens. He gently fed them, feeling something paternal inside him that he hadn't felt in a very long time, not since he was a kid with a puppy of his own. "Maybe I need to look into a shelter or a nonprofit who donates to a shelter or getting volunteers to work in shelters or something like that," he muttered.

"Obviously you love animals," Talia noted beside him.

He nodded. "What's not to love?"

"But loving and *love-ing*," she pointed out, "are two very different things."

"I know what you mean." He smiled. "It's been one of those days. … It's been one of those weeks."

"You want to tell me about it?"

"Yeah, I would love to. Maybe over dinner? I haven't even had dinner yet."

"Well, it's still early for dinner," she murmured. "We can go later, or we can just pick up something and bring it down here."

He nodded. "I'm really not that hungry yet. I had a really big but late lunch. After a very long talk with my psychiatrist, I went in and had lunch with her. I was quite surprised, but she was more than happy to continue the conversation."

"And it must have been intense if it had to go past your session and into lunch," she murmured.

"I guess so," he replied. "It's weird how something happens, and only then do you realize just how much you need to get it off your chest."

"I'm glad she's a help."

"She's a huge help, and I would be the first to say that I've never looked forward to any of those sessions, and I never thought that I ever would. Yet now I see how a lot can be said for it."

She smiled. "Good. In that case, it sounds as if everything is happening as it's meant to."

"I hope so." He looked over at her. "How was your day?'

"Not bad, crazy busy though."

"That just never seems to end though, does it?"

"No, it doesn't," she murmured. "Even though we try hard."

He laughed. "I know. It's just something that we have to consider all the time."

"How did your meeting with Shane go?" she asked point-blank.

He glanced at her, and his lips quirked. "Shane is a bigger man than I am. You told me that he would take me back but not the details."

She raised her eyebrows at that. "Meaning?"

"Meaning, he wasn't looking for an apology. He wasn't looking for anything along that line. He was just looking for me to say that I wanted him to go to work again on my team. That I would work with him, not against him."

"And, of course, it's never quite that easy," she murmured.

"Not only is it not easy, but he's very busy. So I think

we worked it out, and I think he'll be back on my team, at least that was my request, and he's agreed to it. He has to shuffle some things and some people around though."

"Right," she noted, "so it might be a little crazy until the next couple of patients leave."

He frowned. "I wondered about that. I feel bad because of Mandy, but I don't feel bad because of Mandy."

She laughed. "Although that was clear as mud, I still understood."

"You see? That's the nice thing about you," Xavier shared. "Even when things are as clear as mud, and I'm kidding, you still get it."

"Oh, I don't know that I *always* get it," she clarified, "but, as long as you're happy, that's what matters."

He smiled, gave her that grin, and replied, "Let's just say that I feel as if a huge weight's off my shoulder. I feel as if I have finally retraced some steps, and maybe, just maybe, I'll have a chance to …" He waited, trying to gather his thoughts and then shrugged. "I've brought up all kinds of stuff, about deserving the good stuff and putting in a lot of the military training and putting your friends and your buddies first and making sure that nobody gets left behind," he shared. "I hadn't realized how much of that I'd internalized and had taken to heart."

"It sounds as if it was not necessarily the wrong thing to take to heart."

"No, maybe not," he admitted, "but it doesn't mean it was the right thing either. Or that in different circumstances the meanings are different."

She nodded slowly. "I can see that. Obviously a lot of relationship stuff exists between you and Zander."

"Yes, and Zander has had yet another setback, and he

can't come here until he's stabilized."

"No, of course not." She winced. "I'm sorry. It's hard to move away, hard to move forward, hard to take that step that you need to do when other people who are important to you can't do it with you. But you still need to do it anyway."

"Exactly," he conceded, with that sad smile. "I've had lots of talks with Zander, lots of talks with the shrinks, and essentially nothing's changed. I feel better now that I've sorted out Shane, and I feel better now that I can eat again," he explained. "My stomach is obviously very stress-oriented, and it's been giving me fits and starts this last little bit."

"And maybe that's a good thing," she suggested. "Maybe all of that's a good thing."

"Oh, it's a good thing in one way," he agreed, "but it's not such a good thing in another way. It's adjustments, right? But Shane has forgiven me. I am working on forgiving myself. That was partly what my shrink session was all about. Zander says there was never anything to forgive," Xavier stated, with a smile. "And to keep his place warm because he's coming here. He just has to get past an infection he's working on right now."

"He sounds like a fighter."

"That's Zander all the way. He'll go down fighting each and every time, but he'll also get back up when you think that there is absolutely no more getting back up."

"Well, he sounds like somebody we could certainly help here then."

"Absolutely. I just have to get him here."

"No, *you* don't."

He frowned at her and then slowly nodded. "Right. *I* don't have to get him here. There's a place for him here, if and when he's well enough to travel."

"Exactly, so that's not your fault."

"No." He took a deep breath and slowly exhaled. "It's hard letting go of taking care of the world."

"Try working here, watching the patients come and go, only to realize that some will do well, and some won't. Still, it doesn't matter because, once they leave Hathaway House, they're pretty well out of your life."

"I don't know that I could do your job," Xavier noted. He looked down at the kittens in his arms. "And I couldn't do Stan's."

"But yet there are people, like Stan and me, who enjoy our jobs. So, I couldn't do the job that you did, and now that you're rehabbing to be free and clear to do whatever you want again," she suggested, "you should find something that makes you totally happy."

He laughed. "*Happy.* I thought that was pushing Zander to do his best and to ensure that he was coming here."

"And what about before that?"

"Before that I was working on getting my life together again," he said, with a laugh.

"And have you? Got it together?"

"No, obviously not. Am I partway there? Yes."

"I'm sure Hathaway wants you to spend some time working on that and not worrying about all the rest that seems so overwhelmingly necessary at times."

"If only."

She nodded. "It's not a case of *if only*. It's a case of *just make it happen.*"

He smiled at her. "Not a bad goal."

"It's a good goal," she murmured. "And one that you would do well to put as a priority."

He nodded. "Maybe I can make that happen too. …

Just a lot going on in my world."

"True. Just don't rush to solve any of it."

"It would be nice to think so," he replied, relaxing back and smiling up at her. "As long as you're not in any rush."

"I'm not in any rush," she said. "I'm not going anywhere."

He stared at her shrewdly. "You really will be here for the long term?"

"Yes. This is where my heart is. This is where my work is. This is where I feel as if I can contribute."

He stared off in the distance and nodded. "That makes something easier."

"What?" she asked.

He shook his head. "I'm not quite ready to go there yet. Soon, but just not yet."

"Why don't you try *not* going anywhere right now?" she suggested. "Just be you. Find a way to be happy."

"That's what I'm doing," he confirmed. "I'll spend the next weeks just focusing on having Shane's help and not being a jerk about it and trying to get as good as I can get," he shared. "At the same time I'm tossing around some ideas, things that make me happy."

He reached out a hand, gently disentangling it from the kitten in his arms. She took it easily. He continued. "Just want to let you know that you're one of those things that makes me very happy."

She smiled. "I'm glad to hear that because you make me very happy too."

He chuckled. "I'm really glad to hear that, especially when I've been such a jerk."

"You haven't been a jerk," she corrected. "That's the thing for you to remember. You've just been dealing with things."

"*Great.*" He gave her an eye roll, and then he burst out laughing. "Nope, it has been me, but I have come a long way in a very short time." He sighed. "I won't say it's been easy or it's been simple, but I'm feeling a lot more like the old me."

"And maybe *the old me* is pretty perfect too," she noted.

Just then Robin came back and held out her hands for the kittens. Talia returned her two, and Xavier handed his over gently.

Robin added, "You know you can always come back to offer a helping hand, right?"

He nodded. "I know, but it's now a time issue."

"For all of us." Robin laughed and watched as the two of them left.

Chapter 15

SEVERAL DAYS LATER Talia stopped in Xavier's room and asked, "Hey, how about dinner on the deck tonight?"

"Sounds good," he replied.

She smiled at him. "You seem to be a lot more adjusted. As a matter of fact," she murmured, "a lot more at peace."

He nodded. "Absolutely. Definitely more peace in my world now. Thanks for noticing."

She eyed him. "You can't be at peace without someone noticing it?"

"Well, I wasn't there before, but it's coming on now."

"Good, and that's all your doing."

"I don't know," he said, with a big smile. "I don't think I'm quite that good at it."

"You'll get better as time goes on."

"That's definitely happening," he agreed, "and it's interesting to see the change."

"Good," she murmured. "I'll meet you back here at your room at the end of the day." And, with that, she dashed off.

Work was crazy busy with patients coming and going. One thing that she did get set up was an interview for Yvonne. It was a couple days off yet, but Talia was looking forward to meeting her. Anyone important to Dennis was somebody who Talia wanted to see. She was sorry it hadn't worked out for them. Yet she didn't really want to spend too much time dwelling on that because she was too busy dwelling on spending time with Xavier, hoping their relationship would work out. Maybe it was selfish of her, but it was hard to think of anything else for most of her day. So it was a good thing that she was always just busy, busy, busy.

At the end of the day she walked down the hallway to see if Xavier was ready.

He looked up from his bed and smiled at her. "Hey, I've been waiting for you."

"Sorry, it's just been completely nuts today."

"Hey, no problem," he murmured. "Remember? I get it."

"You do get it." She laughed. "I'm grateful."

He smiled and stood up, grabbed a single walking stick she hadn't noticed propped up beside him, and waved her toward the door. "Let's go."

Talia gasped. Went to hug him but stopped midstep. "Wow."

He gave her a huge grin and took a few steps in front of her.

She frowned. "Are you supposed to go straight from a wheelchair to walking? Just like that? No crutches?"

Xavier laughed. "Shane okayed it. And of course I've been doing a lot of practicing during our sessions. This is my maiden voyage to the dining room. Then I eat and rest and walk back to my room, hopefully without falling or tripping. Plus, report back to Shane of course."

"I'm so proud of you. Wow."

"I didn't want to tell you and then get so nervous that I couldn't carry out this exercise in full. Is that okay with you? Do you understand why I did that?"

"Yes. Yes, of course. You do what works best for you.

You've really come back around, after a few setbacks. Wow."

As they headed down the hallway, he grabbed her hand in his.

She smiled, tears in her eyes. When he saw them and seemed worried, she added, "*Happy* tears."

They headed hand in hand down the hallway, enjoying each other's company.

Xavier shared, "Shane was saying that some new staff members were coming in."

"I'm not surprised," Talia muttered. "The work is pretty steady, and we could all use some additional help."

"I get it," he murmured.

"How about you?" she asked. "So more progress?"

"Definite progress now," he replied, "and all because of Shane."

"And Shane would say it's all because of you."

"Exactly," Shane agreed, from behind them. "I mean, look at him. His strength is coming back. He's walking easier. He's standing easier."

"I know," Xavier agreed. "I'm starting to sleep now too."

"And you're eating," Dennis added in a crowing tone, as they all got in line at the buffet. Dennis was so proud, as if he'd single-handedly turned around all of Xavier's food issues.

"Stress," Shane noted. "It'll get you every time." And he quickly separated from them and headed over to meet a group of people who were waiting for him.

"He's really busy, isn't he?" Xavier noted.

She nodded. "Very," she murmured. "And he doesn't begrudge the time. He knows that he just has to apply himself a little harder in order to get everybody the way he wants them. He doesn't want to see anybody get shipped out in less-than-perfect condition."

"Oh, I would be happy with even close to perfect," Xavier said, with a laugh.

"Don't tell him that," Talia said. "Shane will think you're cutting yourself short."

"Not intentionally," Xavier replied. "It's just you don't know what to even ask for or what you can have after these injuries. Then, all of a sudden, everybody here tells you how you can have the world, and it doesn't even seem possible. Then you see others who are getting it, and you want it yourself."

"Sounds as if you're almost there," Talia pointed out, smiling.

"I'm certainly a lot closer than I was. I think I've only got another month or two here."

She stopped in the line and turned to look at him. "What?" she asked, her voice shaky. She hadn't realized that his time was coming to an end so soon. They'd been in this little la-la land of their own making, not even understanding that this was coming to an end so fast.

He smiled at her gently. "Yeah. It kinda came as a shock to me too. I have to settle up all kinds of issues, like where I'll go from here."

She nodded slowly. "And where do you want to go?"

"I'll stay local. I'm signing up for their weekend program that goes on after this," he added. "I don't dare *not* continue with my PT training—at least for a while."

"Of course," she said, the relief in her tone obvious.

He chuckled. "Yeah, we haven't exactly discussed what comes after this, have we?"

"No. I was quite happy to be blinded by the fact that you would always be here."

"And yet that can't happen."

"Of course. … Of course I know that. I mean, intellectually I know that."

"Hey, I'm in the same boat. It just hit home when we turned the page on the calendar."

She nodded. "Funny how time goes by, and you don't even realize it."

"And then all of a sudden you look up, and it's September, and I've been here some four-plus months."

"Wow, she whispered.

XAVIER SMILED GENTLY at Talia and added, "But I'm not leaving anytime soon."

"I don't know," she muttered. "The time goes by so fast."

"Maybe," he murmured. "But, if I'm only moving into town, it's not bad."

"That's true," she said, brightening.

"I presume we can still see each other."

She nodded.

But she knew, and he knew, it would be different because how could it not be? Here, they saw each other multiple times a day. Once he left, that couldn't continue. Once he was good enough to go, he had to go. That was a fact of life. But he also knew it would be hard to leave her, something that he wasn't necessarily ready for. But, if it was time for him to leave, then it was time. He had to trust the process that there was something else afterward for him. For him with Talia.

"I'll be working with Lance in town for a while," he told

her. "See what I want to do. I have benefits for quite a while. It's not as there's an end date on them. I just want to figure out my next career, something that I'll enjoy doing."

"And I certainly agree with that," she said. "I would love to think of you doing something that would make you smile every day."

"*You* make me smile every day," he replied, chuckling.

She flushed. "And I'm really glad to hear that, but you do need something more too."

"Ooh, trying to get rid of me already?" he teased.

"That is the last thing I'm trying to do," she stated. She grabbed his hand. "I'm really happy with the way things have turned out for you."

He smiled at her and looked down at their joined hands. "Me too. I just hope that you're not too anxious to see the end of me."

"No, not at all," she declared. "I'll probably burst into tears when that day comes."

He looked at her. "Why?"

"Because things will change," she said. "Everything will change."

"Everything always changes," he replied gently.

"I know that, in theory, and I'll be gloriously happy for you, … but that won't mean that I won't be sad at the change in our own circumstances."

He nodded. "Which is also another reason why I'll stay in town. I really don't want to lose touch with you."

She smiled through her suddenly blurry eyes.

He gently wiped away a tear. "No tears," he whispered. "I'm not leaving for quite a while."

"I'm glad to hear that, and I'm hoping your friend will make it here before then."

"If I stay close, and Zander does get in, then I'll see him and help him in any way that I can. And, if he doesn't make it in, I've done everything I can for him, but obviously it was time for a change."

She smiled at that. "That's definitely a change of attitude."

"Only out of necessity." Xavier chuckled. "Now look. Dennis is waiting for us."

And they stepped up to grab their dinners.

Chapter 16

TALIA BURIED HERSELF in her work over the next few weeks, trying to avoid what she knew would be a very difficult time coming up.

Even Dani asked her about it. "Hey, are you okay?"

"Yeah. … It was just brought home to me that he'll be leaving soon."

Dani nodded sympathetically. "Right? It's amazing how much we can get adjusted to the system that we have going on here, without looking at how it'll have to change moving forward."

"I wasn't even thinking that *I* would have to change," she admitted, with a sad smile. "I guess I was living in la-la land, thinking he would stay here forever."

Dani gave her an odd look.

Talia raised both hands in surrender. "Don't. … Don't even look at me like that. I get it. That was so foolish."

"It's not foolish," Dani argued, "but obviously you'll struggle when he leaves."

"Yep, I sure will. Yet it doesn't make a whole lot of sense because he's staying close in town."

Dani raised her eyebrows. "That's huge."

"I know, but it's not quite the same as his being here beside me all the time."

"No, of course not," Dani murmured. At that she smiled

and added, "Yet sometimes that change is really good."

"It will be for him. And I'll still see him. It's just *different.*"

Dani nodded and went back to work, leaving Talia alone with her thoughts. She didn't even know how to or what to think about any of this, so she just basically put it out of her mind and kept on working. Even seeing him daily, she was surprised to see a marked change in his stride, to see him walking so strong. "Wow, look at that progress."

He nodded. "And it feels good too."

"And it should," she declared, staring at him. "That's huge."

"Well, I don't know about the *huge* part, but it's definitely progress that, for a long time, I wondered I would even make."

"Obviously you have, and you have dealt with that quite nicely."

He chuckled. "Enough is going on in my world right now that it's still in many ways one day forward and one day backward."

She raised an eyebrow. "Meaning?"

"Just like you noted, there's a change. I've got a meeting with Lance coming up," he shared. "He's popping by."

"Yep, he does that a lot."

Xavier nodded. "I'm looking forward to it, just checking out what I might do once I leave here. I'll get an apartment in town that's close enough to the gym that I can continue to work out, to slowly build up my muscles. I'll sign up for the weekend rehab sessions here too. Meanwhile I will figure out what I want to do for a job, if anything."

"*If anything* is an option," she noted, "then at least you can just focus on healing for now."

"That's what I was thinking," he said. "I don't want to take anything too far, too fast, and I don't want to stress myself out at this point."

She agreed with everything he said, but it was still hard to realize that that endpoint was speeding toward them.

AT DINNERTIME THE next day, Xavier asked Talia, "Are you okay?"

She nodded. "I am." Then she took a deep breath. "It's just hard."

"It is," he murmured, "but that's all right. These are *good* changes. The meeting with Lance went well. I'm just gathering ideas about a future job for me. Plus, the latest testing with Shane went well. It's amazing to see the progress I've made since day one here. I'm improving greatly, even from my viewpoint." He shook his head. "I have signed up for some of the weekend PT workshops here, so I'll be here on an irregular basis. And, of course, otherwise I'm a whole fifteen minutes away."

"I know," she muttered, "and *yet* fifteen minutes."

He laughed. "I know. I get it. It's different."

"It's a funny thing, but even fifteen minutes seems as if it's too much separation from you."

"Fifteen minutes can be too much," he agreed, "but I don't have a car yet, and I have to get a new driver's license and a few other problems taken care of before I can get here."

She stared at him. "Right, I didn't even think about that."

"That's because you're not the one who has to move out

and to become an adult again," he noted, chuckling.

"Oh, even when you put it that way, it brings back horrible memories."

"Of course it does. Growing up and the growing pains that come with it," he said, a big smile on his face. "But essentially I have to be adept enough to leave home again."

"You're doing so well that it won't be a problem."

"I don't think it'll be a problem," he clarified, "but you can't ever really count on anything that's in progress," he cautioned. "You don't want it to be a problem, yet ..." And he just left it at that.

She understood. Still it was amazingly difficult to even think about him leaving. However, she could hope that, as long as everybody was working and doing their jobs, Xavier would progress to that next stage of life quite naturally, and anything that he had to adapt to would be easy. "Are you looking forward to having a place of your own again?"

"I'm looking forward to a lot of things," he admitted. "And, yes, peace and quiet, privacy, all that is definitely part of it, but I will miss the food at Hathaway House."

She smiled. "Maybe you should take some cooking classes."

"That's not a bad idea. It would be good for me. I'm not a great cook."

She shrugged. "I'm not either."

He chuckled. "And here I thought you would save me from myself."

"Nope. You should take the cooking classes though. I'm all in favor of that."

He smiled. "That sounds like a doable thing. It even sounds like fun. I was talking to Ilse a little bit about it, and she had a couple suggestions."

"Really?"

"Sure, it's her field."

"It is, indeed." Talia smiled. "Funny how I never even thought of that."

Xavier shrugged. "It makes sense that the chef here would know where the good cooking classes are and what to start with."

"I guess when you were in the navy, you had a lot of cooking done for you too, right?"

"Absolutely. I can do just fine on a barbecue pit, but I think it's time I learned a little bit more than that."

She smiled. "I don't even barbecue much."

"Ah, so, in other words, I'll be doing the cooking when we're together, is that it?" he asked in a teasing voice.

"Hey, if you can cook, then it's all on you," she declared, chuckling.

"We'll see," he said. "I'm not sure how much I can cook. And that's one of the things that I'm looking forward to finding out. It's a weird stage of life for me. I'm looking forward to having a barbecue and to learning to cook on my own again."

Even later she was thinking about his words because it wasn't exactly anything she'd thought about. She didn't really cook, and she hadn't really needed to, not with the food here being so awesome and available. It was a perk of working here. So that wasn't much of an issue at all. Still, she might want to cook in her own kitchen, to create things from scratch, and maybe it would be nice to have more of those skills.

She thought about it a lot over the next few days and told Xavier, "I've been thinking about the cooking classes."

"Good." He smiled. "You want to take some with me?"

She stared at him. "What?"

He smiled. "Didn't even occur to you, did it?"

"You caught me with a couple things," she explained. "The whole *taking a class together* thing, which I think is a good idea, was one of the biggest things. Yet even taking a class solo wasn't something that I really had on my radar."

"Maybe it should be," he said.

"Oh, it definitely should be," she murmured. "I just hadn't really considered it."

"And that's part of what I'm doing right now," he shared. "I'm thinking about everything. I have lots to figure out regarding what I'm supposed to do with my life at this stage. I'm not very comfortable with change," he shared, "yet I know an awful lot of opportunity is here for growth."

"And I'm all for it. I think it's a heck of an idea."

He smiled. "I'm really glad to hear that, so sign up with me."

She nodded. "What kind of a cooking class is it?"

"I found a bunch of them. A basics class for people like me, who don't know very much," he shared, "also ones like Chinese and Indian specialities."

"Hey, I'm all for something like that too," she agreed. "I wonder if Ilse would give us any of her recipes here for some of our favorite foods?"

He stared at her. "It's worth asking."

She shrugged. "If I ever were to leave my onsite apartment, then I would more likely ask. In the meantime it seems like it would be the wrong thing to do."

"I'm not sure there is a wrong thing to do here," he noted, chuckling. "It seems as if you guys are all about acceptance."

"Ooh, we are," she agreed.

"And that's a really good point too. Besides, if you spend more time with me, we'll do a lot more cooking together, so it would be fun to learn together."

"I absolutely love that idea," she said warmly. "Kinda surprised I didn't even think of it myself."

"That's because it's comfortable here for you. I mean, think about it. You don't *have* to do any cooking."

She nodded. "It's a weird thing, isn't it? Not many jobs have these meals as perks."

"It's a good thing in many ways, but, for somebody like me, who wants to learn to cook, it can be a bit daunting."

"Of course. For me too," she admitted. "Still, I'm quite stoked over the idea."

"Good. I'll send you a bunch of options, so we can figure out which classes we want to take."

She nodded enthusiastically.

Chapter 17

WHEN TALIA MENTIONED it to Dani a few days later, Dani raised her eyebrows. "What a great idea. I wonder if anybody here wants cooking classes. I imagine that, as a life skill, cooking classes would be something that a lot of people could use, patients and staff alike. … It never even occurred to me. I don't cook myself much at all," she shared, with an eye roll. "I mean, when you think about it, it's not something that we have to do here. Plus, when we do cook at home, it's more like throw your own steak on the barbecue and go from there."

"Very true," Talia agreed, smiling. "Also an interesting way to look at the stressors that these guys all have to deal with, once they are no longer at Hathaway House."

"For anybody who doesn't know how to cook, that's an added stress to leaving here, which is already stressful, and we don't want them to fail so …" Dani was nodding. "I might talk to Ilse about that. We won't get anything in place for Xavier before he leaves here, but we can get it started for others hopefully."

"Xavier leaving is coming up so fast and is already causing *me* no end of stress."

"Of course it is," Dani noted gently. "But I think you two taking cooking classes together will be huge."

"I hope so. It's such a funny thing to even realize that I

can't cook, and neither can he, and here he's the one who signed up to do something about it."

"And I love that," Dani declared. "I really do. I love to see the initiative happening."

So did Talia, but it was something so obvious that once again it surprised her. She hadn't really considered the cooking issues for her or for the patients here. Now that it had been identified, it was a glaring difference between the way her and Xavier's minds worked. And she wasn't even sure if that was a good thing or a bad thing. As it was, it didn't really matter because it was already in progress. And the two of them cheerfully picked out three different courses—one a weekend workshop, and the two others were evening classes.

Xavier asked her, "You'll be okay to do evenings?"

She nodded. "I'll be just fine to do evenings."

"Good, because a bunch of other stuff is offered in town that I was hoping maybe I could take you to."

She smiled at him. "Like what?"

"I don't know how you feel about sports games, but a few of them I would like to see. Also I haven't been to the movies in a long time. ... Such a strange feeling, having these options, almost like having a new lease on life."

"I don't know about a *strange* feeling," she replied, "but sounds like a wonderful feeling to me."

He smiled. "See? I like that. You're always up for something new."

"Of course. And I haven't necessarily been great about going forward and learning things that I need to learn on my own," she noted, "but you've really opened my eyes too. You've got a real gung-ho attitude, and I'm really enjoying that."

He smiled. "So, if we are doing these classes, particularly something on a weekend, would you be okay to stay overnight at my place?"

She nodded. "It would make a lot more sense than driving back and forth daily—as long as you get a place that's big enough."

"Right. That'll be a big priority."

"Of course, but not just that. I'm sure you would like to have much more in your world too."

He grinned. "So many different things would be fun to do," he shared, "and to know that I have you there to share it with is major."

As the days went on, she found that she was getting more and more … not upset, just short-tempered and easily distracted.

Finally Dani called her in and said, "Hey, obviously you're struggling with something."

"And I shouldn't be," she muttered. "It's stupid."

"*But …*" Dani nudged her.

"*But* he's moving out in a few days."

Dani understood. "Right. And you fear those changes will be the end of your relationship."

"No, no, not at all," Talia countered. "That's why I feel so stupid. And I don't mean to bother you or to disturb you with any of this. … And I'm sorry I've been so distracted."

Dani held up a hand. "Stop. I'm talking to you as a friend, not as an employer. Obviously something is upsetting you, and I needed to find out what."

"The *what* is just plain stupid," she admitted, "because we've already booked cooking classes together. So obviously him leaving Hathaway House is not the end. Still, it just, … well, it feels as if it's the end."

"Well, it's the end as you currently know it," Dani clarified.

"Maybe that's it," Talia conceded, with a nod. "And I guess I'm not handling the idea that another beginning is in here."

"Beginnings are good though," Dani reminded her.

"Maybe, but they're also hard. And it feels very much as if he might find a whole new world out there, and maybe I won't be a part of it."

Dani stared at her. "Oh, wow. So really it has absolutely nothing to do with the fact that he's leaving but the fact that you feel very insecure in the relationship."

Nonplussed, that insight sent light bulbs going off in her head. "And that's just foolish, isn't it?"

"I don't know that it's foolishness, so much as I think it's probably a fairly normal reaction," Dani replied, with a gentle smile. "And, of course, you're nervous and, of course, you're worried. You're probably also worried about how he'll make out while he's out there in the big bad world."

"Sure. Yet it's funny because I expect him to do really well."

"Maybe too well?" Dani asked, with another shrewd insight.

"And that would be just terrible if that's what I was expecting," Talia admitted, with a heavy sigh. "Why do we do this to ourselves?"

"Because we care," Dani said instantly. "And caring is never wrong."

Talia smiled. "You're right there. It doesn't feel *wrong*. It just feels *very strange*."

"Strange isn't bad either," Dani murmured. "All you really need is to feel better about where you both are. And if that were resolved, then you would not be so nervous about him leaving.”

“That sounds theoretically logical,” Talia noted cautiously. “I guess I need to talk to him.”

“Well, somebody needs to,” Dani said, laughing. “And obviously you’re the best person.”

And again, she winced at that. “And again, I’m sorry.”

“Don’t,” Dani repeated. “No apologies are necessary here. We got it. You’re in a state of uncertainty over a relationship that really matters to you. Believe me that we’ve all been there.”

“I know, but you’re on the other side of that. And everything is really going well for you.”

Dani nodded. “We’ve moved up the wedding date,” she shared, her cheeks turning pink.

Talia stared at her in shock. “What?”

“Not only that, he’s been doing double the course load to get back here full-time as soon as he can. And it’s been working. He’ll graduate earlier than we expected.”

“Wow.” Talia stared at Dani. “That’s huge news.”

“It is. It won’t happen in the next month or two, but I have hopes that maybe, not too long after that, it will be a done deal. He’ll be working here, and we’ll be married.”

“You’ve waited quite a while,” Talia murmured, “so I’m really happy that it’s working out for you.”

“And yours will work out too,” Dani stated firmly. “But obviously you guys still have some insecurities to work through.”

“I certainly do,” she said, with a wry smile. “And it just makes me feel even more foolish.”

Dani shook her head. “And again, that’s ridiculous. When you care, it’s easy to get hurt, and what you’re trying to do is *not* get hurt by already prepping yourself in case things don't work out."

"That just sounds terrible." Talia shuddered.

"I don't think it's even so much *terrible*," Dani corrected, "as much as I think it's just your self-defense mechanism kicking in. Just in case things don't work out, you'll be happy for him anyway."

"Of course I will be," she muttered.

"But what you really want is for things to work out for you two."

"Yes, absolutely." She looked over at Dani and winced. "I really love him," she whispered. "I didn't think it would ever happen."

"I know you love him. It's obvious. But I don't think you've told him that."

"No, I haven't," she replied. "I'm not any good at that stuff."

Dani's laughter pealed out bright and strong. "I think everybody would say that. When it comes to matters of the heart, some people find it very easy to talk about, while others don't."

"I come in the *don't* category," Talia declared bluntly. "I figure that's because I've never had any practice at it."

"I don't know that having practice makes for success or not here," Dani pointed out. "So maybe this is to your benefit."

"I don't know," Talia muttered. "It just feels so wrong in so many ways."

"And yet you're doing a great job here, and you're doing a great job with him," Dani said, "so you just need to trust a little bit more."

"Maybe," she muttered. "And I can't have it showing up

at work. I am so sorry for that."

"And again, you need to stop with the apologies," Dani stated firmly. "I was just checking in to see how things were going because obviously you're distracted."

And, with that, Talia thanked her boss, her friend, and headed back to her desk. Leaving her feeling even worse. Yes, she had been distracted. Maybe Dani was right. Maybe Talia had been automatically making excuses in case things didn't work out with Xavier, just to let herself off the hook. Excuses like, *It wasn't meant to be. Things like that just didn't happen to her. There was no way to know. He would get out in the big bad world and find it so much better than what he'd thought that he wouldn't want her.*

All these worrisome thoughts going through her head, and she knew it wasn't fair. He hadn't in any way made any indication or sign that he was even thinking along that line. But she was automatically giving him that out, just in case. She sighed, a heavy difficult sigh.

Shane popped into her office and said, "I heard that."

She looked up, frowned, then shrugged. "Of course you did. How is he doing today?"

"He's having a whole series of good days," Shane replied, with a smile. "He'll be remarkably in good shape when leaving here."

She winced at that. "I'm really happy to hear that," she muttered.

"And yet somehow I'm not sure that you and I are looking at this from the same perspective."

She stared at him. "Meaning?"

"Meaning that, when I say he'll be in remarkably good shape, that's supposed to bring a smile to your face."

"It is," she conceded. Then, giving up the ghost, she

added, "I'm really happy for him, but he's leaving, and that'll always be a hard thing for me."

"And yet all he talks about is the fact that you guys have signed up for some cooking classes together and other outings that he's really excited about."

She smiled. "I'm really glad to hear that too." Yet she frowned, shook her head. "And you're right. We have made future plans. And that, in a way, is also making me a little nervous."

"Nervous of a commitment?" Shane asked.

"Not on my side," she replied, "but I almost feel as if maybe he needs to be fancy-free and footloose to go do his thing, without me around."

"Ouch," Shane muttered. "I honestly don't think that is a very good idea at all."

She looked at him. "Why?"

"Because he's planning a future with you," Shane pointed out. "You get that, right?"

She stared at him. "We're … We haven't got that far."

"No, you haven't, but that doesn't mean that that's not where it's going."

"I would hope that's where it's going," she said. "And, yet again, we haven't got that far."

He nodded. "So we're back to the fact that you guys need to sit down and have one of 'those' talks."

"Yeah, maybe one of 'those' talks," she repeated, "but 'those' talks aren't easy to have."

He burst out laughing. "Hey, I'm on the other side of one of 'those' talks," he stated, with a big grin. "And it wasn't easy then either."

She nodded. "So, just because we need to have one of 'those' talks"—she sent him a mocking look—"doesn't mean that I can make that happen anytime soon."

"No, it doesn't, but I think it should happen before he leaves."

"I guess," she muttered. "It's just very uncomfortable."

"Of course it is, and that's because you're assuming that he doesn't feel the same way you do."

"I want him to. He makes it sound as if he does."

"But you don't believe him?"

"It's not that I don't believe him …" Then she frowned.

"But you're not sure," Shane noted. "And, because you're not sure, it's making you like this."

"Maybe," she muttered, raising both hands. "You know that it's all so new."

"Good. That makes it new for both of you."

She stared at him. "Meaning?"

"It's not easy for him either. He's putting a lot on the line because he doesn't see himself necessarily as whole and complete."

"But of course he is," she argued. "Even if he were still in a wheelchair, he would be."

At that, Shane smiled. "That's the thing. You know that, but I'm not sure he believes that."

"That would be just foolish," she stated crossly. "I've told him."

Shane started to laugh. "Have you told him in just that way? And hasn't he told you some things that make you realize how much he cares?"

"Sure." And then she realized she'd fallen into the trap. She glared at him. "It's different."

"No," he argued gently, but his smile was still in place. "It's not that different at all. It's all about opening up your hearts and seeing if you're both on the same page."

"I thought we were, and now all I have is doubts."

"Doubts about how you feel?"

"No," she declared. "Not at all. Doubts that I'm the right person for him. Doubts that he wouldn't be better off trying life on his own for a while, before he and I get this close."

"Too late," Shane stated, "because you guys are already that close. And don't bother lying about it because I already see it. We all can. We watched this romance blossom for months." He shook his head. "You should be proud, and you should be happy. You should be grateful. And, on top of all of that," he added, "you should curl in delight every time you even think about him."

"That would be a little difficult," she muttered. "I would never get any work done that way. I already think about him all the time anyway."

He grinned. "And that's what I mean. You know how you feel. Now all you need to do is believe in how he feels."

"I thought I was there. Every time I turn around, I'm slapped up against something new and disconcerting."

"Disconcerting is not necessarily a problem," Shane replied. "And it gives you a new chance every time to come up against something else. Something else to deal with."

"Oh, that sounds *lovely*," she quipped, with an eye roll. "Do you really think I need *more* to deal with?"

"Obviously you do," he pointed out, with a bright grin. "Otherwise you wouldn't be in this situation." And, with that, he was gone.

XAVIER WASN'T SURE what was going on with Talia, but she

was a little more distant the closer his end date came. He was getting more and more excited because this was something he had waited for and had worked toward for a very long time. So he wasn't at all sure why she was struggling with it.

During one of his last sessions with Shane, Xavier spoke about it. "So I'm a little confused."

Shane looked over at him. "About what?"

"Why she's backing off."

Shane nodded. "I had a similar conversation with her not all that long ago. And I told her that you guys need to talk to each other."

Immediately Xavier's heart froze. "Is she having … Is somebody else in her life?" he demanded.

Shane looked at him in shock and then started to chuckle. "You see? That's exactly why you guys need to talk. Nobody else is in her life, but she's feeling just as insecure about you as you are about her."

"I don't know why she would be insecure at all. She's gorgeous. She's whole. She's got her pick of men," he admitted. "I've come a long way, but I also know I have a long way still to go."

"You need to have this conversation with her," Shane stated. "And do it before you leave. She's already got enough worries going on in that head of hers."

Xavier frowned, but Shane wouldn't say anything else. And when Xavier made a similar comment to Dani, she made a similar point too. He still wasn't sure what to do about it, so he mentioned it to Dennis.

Dennis shrugged. "That's normal."

"What's normal?" Xavier asked, looking at him in confusion.

"Think about it. She's worried that, once you get out

into the big bad world, you'll forget her."

He stared at him in shock. "But we've made all kinds of future plans. I won't forget her. I'm constantly thinking about her."

"Sure, at this point in time, I think both of you have probably made a lot of plans together for evenings here and weekends there. Yet you haven't talked about what's really important, which is how you feel about each other. And so she's feeling a little insecure. You're heading off into an exciting new world and leaving her behind."

He winced at that. "I'm hardly leaving her behind."

"And yet to her it probably looks that way."

It gave him a lot to think about. At dinner tonight he wanted to broach the subject several times, yet he didn't. And it was really frustrating because he wasn't sure how to go about bringing up the subject.

When she asked him, "What is it, two more days?"

He shook his head. "No," he said gently. "Tomorrow is my last day." He watched as tears sprang to her eyes. And it broke his heart. "I'm not leaving *you*. You know that, right?"

She took a deep breath and nodded. "I get that. It's just … it's foolish." She wiped away her tears and gave him a bright smile. "So what have you got planned for tomorrow? It's your last day, after all."

"Shane will run me through some more tests," he replied. "And my last meeting with my psychologist. I've got paperwork due for Dani," he added, ticking everything off on his list. "It'll be a really busy day."

She nodded. "I mean, how can it not be," she murmured. "I guess that's normal."

"If I get a chance, I'll meet you for lunch. Otherwise we'll have to push everything back until dinner."

"That's okay."

"Oh, and Lance is bringing me a vehicle." Xavier smiled. "My driver's license apparently is fine, after the doctors wrote several letters for me."

"Wow," she said, "that's huge. I'm really happy for you. Things are just moving along so fast."

"Well, it's been what? Six months," he said, chuckling. "But I guess from your perspective, it's fast."

She shrugged. "Doesn't matter whether it's my perspective or not. I am delighted for you."

He looked over at her. "You've been such a strong support for me all this time. I don't know that I would have made it without you."

"You would have made it just fine. I know you would have. You have been an incredible success here."

He shook his head. "We're getting maudlin here, and we have to stop that. Tomorrow will already be a tough-enough day."

"Yeah, it will be, exciting but difficult."

He nodded. "And that's just the way life is sometimes," he murmured.

She didn't know what to say to that apparently because she just fell quiet.

He hated that she was as upset over all this as she appeared to be, because that's not how he wanted to leave this place, or her. And yet he could understand that, for her, it was difficult. It was change, a more exciting beginning for him, whereas her perception was more akin to an unhappy ending. This was one of those things that he had no easy way to prep her for. He was excited, beyond excited, to be honest. This was a huge, huge milestone that he'd worked so hard to reach. Just when he was opening his mouth to say something profound about where they would be together, her phone buzzed.

She looked down at it and groaned. "My timer reminder that I've got to run." She looked up at him and smiled. "I don't know how long this will take."

"Go. I know how much this job means to you. I'll meet up with you later."

She nodded. "I really appreciate that." And then she was gone.

Chapter 18

A S IT WAS, last night had been really busy. So, by the time she'd gotten back to the dining room, it had been ten o'clock. And when she'd texted him to see if he was still awake and wanted to meet, he didn't answer. She frowned at that, but there wasn't any help for it. His last day was coming tomorrow whether she liked it or not, whether she was ready or not. And maybe that's the way it was supposed to be. She didn't know anymore. She was being dragged forward. Ready or not, here it was.

When she got up the next morning, it was hard for her to stay even a little bit sane, with so much going on. And by the time lunch came, she was beyond frazzled.

Dani suggested, "Go get lunch, take a break, go for a walk, spend some time with Xavier if you can."

Talia nodded and bolted to his room, but, of course, he wasn't there. And she remembered how he'd mentioned this would be a pretty busy day ahead of him, so she headed back to the nightmare that awaited her in her office. By the time she was done with all the pressing matters, it was already dinnertime. She sat here at her desk for a long moment, trying to catch her breath.

Dani checked in on her. "You okay?"

"I'm fine, just one of those days."

"It really was, wasn't it?" Dani noted, shaking her head.

"How does this end up always happening?"

Talia laughed. "It doesn't *always* happen. It just happens enough that we never seem to really understand how to get out of it."

"I guess so," Dani conceded, shaking her head. "Still seems as if it *always* happens."

"Maybe it is," she admitted, "but we're getting much better at handling it."

And, with that, Talia headed to Xavier's room, wondering if he was ready for dinner. When she couldn't find any sign of him, she frowned and headed back to her place and had a quick shower, wanting to make the evening as nice and as friendly as possible. She didn't want it to be a night of tears, even though she knew that it would be rough on her. And it was foolish, and she knew that, *blah, blah, blah*. No matter what anybody told her, it still didn't make it any easier.

As she walked to the dining room, wearing a nice flowy dress, Dennis looked up and smiled approvingly.

"Hey, don't you look nice tonight."

She smiled. "No point in making this into a rough evening for him, so I figured I would dress up a little bit."

"I'm glad you did," he said, with an extrabright smile.

She wasn't sure what that meant. "Have you seen him yet?"

"Nope, not yet."

She frowned. "I'll go sit out on the deck and wait for him to show up."

"Do you want coffee?" Dennis asked. "Or maybe some southern lemonade?"

"Lemonade?" she asked.

"Yep, I made a big batch today," he replied. "It's in that

big glass jug over there."

She saw a glass pitcher with a whole pile of fresh fruit in it. She poured herself a glass, tasted it, and filled up her glass again. "It's lovely," she said.

"Glad you like it," he called back. "Dinner is served, if you want to eat now."

"Nope, I'll wait. It's beautiful outside. I'll go sit out there." And, glass in her hand, she headed outside to enjoy the cooler evening.

It really was a beautiful evening. Something was so lovely about that whole fresh air aspect on the deck. Hathaway House was a beautiful place, a location that so many people would absolutely love to have available to them. Of course she had almost became dull to it because she was here all the time, focused too much on work and not enough on the blessings her days brought her. It was sad in a way. She wanted to appreciate things more, and she *should* appreciate more, but somehow it was easy to forget about all these good things.

When she heard a call behind her, she turned and waved. "Hey. I've been waiting for you."

"Good," Xavier said cheerfully. He was shaved and dressed and showered.

"Yeah, I went home and had a shower too. It was just one of those days."

"Mine was good," he shared. "It was exciting. It was busy. It was ... it was just so many things."

There was a nervous edge to his tone that she wasn't used to. "Are you okay?" she asked curiously.

"Yep."

Talia thought his tone was a little too hearty.

He asked, "You want to eat now?"

She nodded. "Soon. I'm just having some lemonade. If you want some, it's over in that glass jar." She watched as he walked—so normal, so happy and healthy, that she felt tears again in her eyes.

When he saw her, he asked, "What's the matter?"

"I was just thinking about how far you've come," she whispered, "and you walk, as if it's nothing."

"Well, it's not *nothing*," he clarified. "It's definitely something that I've been working on."

"You've come so far that it's lovely to see."

"It is, indeed," he agreed. "I've come so far, and yet, in some ways, I still haven't come far enough with some things."

"In what things?"

"Well, I'm not really good about expressing my feelings," he admitted. "I'm not really good with locking things down."

"Why do you have to lock anything down?" she asked curiously.

"Because sometimes other people need me to lock things down too," he replied.

"You're supposed to be doing stuff for *you*," she stated, studying him. "That's what you're here for, to improve your life."

He smiled. "Yep, and things don't always work out the way we expect it to be."

She could see that. She looked at the drink in his hand. "Isn't that lemonade good?" she asked.

He nodded. "I've had it a couple times, and every time it always surprises me with just how both sweet and tart it is."

"I think it's supposed to be that way," she teased, "but what do I know?"

He chuckled. "I think you know a heck of a lot. And it's been such a lovely time getting to know you." At that comment, he saw her withdrawing. "And, no, this a *not* goodbye or anything else that your mind might dream up."

She relaxed slightly. "Good. … You can't get rid of me that easily."

"I'm kinda hoping that that's true," he said.

She looked at him in confusion.

He took a deep breath. "One of the things that I think we need to talk about is our future."

Instinctively she tensed. Then she slowly relaxed. "It would probably be a good thing," she noted cautiously. "Depending on what you're planning on saying."

He burst out laughing. "Right? As long as we don't do anything to hurt each other or to harm anyone."

"Right, that would be very ugly. But providing that we're not dealing with any issues like that, I'm more than happy to talk about our future and feelings or whatever it is that you want to bring up."

He looked over at her, a smile playing on the corner of his lips. "Are you though?" he asked.

She stared at him. "I think so, unless it's something that I'm not prepared for."

"I don't think we're ever prepared for this stuff. I know I'm definitely not," he said.

At that, she just looked confused again.

He chuckled. "I'm making a mess of this."

"I don't know what you're making a mess of because I don't understand anything at this moment."

"And that's because just so much is going on in my world right now that I'm not being terribly clear."

"Okay, so let's try for clarity then," she suggested, with a note of humor.

He burst out laughing, and then, in the most casual of tones, he began, "There is something I've been meaning to ask you."

"Yep, what's that?" she asked, looking at him curiously.

He took a deep breath. "This." And he reached in his pocket and grabbed something. Then showed her a tiny little soda can pull tab.

She looked at it curiously. "Is that from a can of soda?"

"It's meant to be a substitute for a point in time when it's not a substitute."

She looked at him uncomprehendingly.

"This is yet another time when I'm just not very good with communication."

"You're doing fine so far. Explain it to me," she replied.

He grinned at her encouragement. "See? There you are again, always trying to help me do better."

"Not *do* better," she said. "Just to keep trying."

"Right. And that's what I'm trying to do. Just bear with me for a second."

She studied him for a moment, while he marshaled his thoughts.

"The question I have to ask is …" He took a deep breath and let it out slowly. "Will you marry me?"

THERE, HE'D DONE it. He got it out. He watched the expressions on her face—the shock, the awareness, the understanding now of the pop can ring in the palm of his hand. And, oh dear God, she wasn't answering.

Then she whispered, "Are you sure?" she asked. "No

take-backs are allowed here."

He stared at her and then started to chuckle. "I don't want any take-backs, sweetheart. I love you. I always have."

Her eyes filled with tears, and he was afraid she would start to bawl on the spot. "But I really could use an answer." And he hated that such nervousness filled his tone that anybody close by would hear it.

Talia threw her arms around him, held him close, and whispered, "Yes, yes, yes, a thousand times yes."

He stood and picked her up in his arms and twirled her around. And then he stopped, looked down at her, and muttered, "Do you realize what I just did?"

She laughed. "Yes, I do. You picked me up, and you twirled me around, just like any healthy guy would do."

He picked her up again, hugged her tight, and whispered, "And thank God you gave the right answer."

And with a solemness that he hadn't expected to feel, he placed the pop can ring on her finger and vowed, "We will exchange this when we get to town, and you can buy whatever ring you would absolutely love to wear."

"Thank you," she whispered, "but we're also keeping this forever too."

His smile burst free. "Now, you want to try for that yes again?"

She threw her arms around his neck and proclaimed loudly, "Yes!"

He lowered his head, and he kissed her gently through the din and the noise. In the background, he heard caterwauling going on. He lifted his head to look around, and the entire kitchen staff, plus what seemed to be the entire population of Hathaway House, were all grinning and clapping and cheering. They wore party hats and had wrapped streamers around their necks. The element of creative surprise was at work here. He nudged her and said, "Look at this."

She turned and gasped in shock, her face turning adorably pink, as she realized everybody had watched and had heard. "Oh my God," she muttered, her hands on her cheeks. "Is Dennis responsible for the party decorations?"

"Of course," Dani said. "You think any of us would miss out on that?" She walked over and gave Talia a big hug. "Congratulations."

"Thank you," she whispered, tears in her eyes. "Thank you so much."

After that came Dennis and Shane, and it seemed as if the hugs just went on forever.

And finally Dennis announced, "And now we have champagne for the happy couple to have a proper celebration." He brought out bubbly for the two of them. "And dinner is ready."

With that, he served them a full three-course meal, wouldn't let them get up for anything, and explained, "It's your night. After this, you are on your own, as you've graduated, Xavier. Believe me that's a huge milestone you need to celebrate each and every day," he declared cheerfully. "But tonight, you get waited on. It's the least I can do."

And, with that, the two of them sat there marveling, as Dennis served them a meal that was better than any five-star restaurant anywhere.

Talia grabbed Xavier's hand and whispered, "Thank you."

He asked her, "For what?"

"For talking to me first, before you left," she said. "It was killing me to know you were leaving, and we hadn't had a relationship talk. I was planning on talking to you about it tonight, but I'm so relieved that you got there first."

He smiled. "I figured if we got the basics out of the way, everything else would fall into place."

"I think it did." She chuckled. "And I'm grateful that having you nearby means I get to stay here."

"Absolutely. The work done here is way too important not to have you still be a part of it. I also know it's where your heart is. I'll figure mine out as I go along," he added, "but not to worry. We won't be destitute."

"I'm not even worried about that," she said. "Some things are way more important."

"Like what?" he asked.

She smiled through her tears. "*Love*. Love trumps everything. And, in case I didn't tell you before, I really love you. And I am so looking forward to the rest of our life."

"I love you, Talia." Not a whole lot more he could say, choked with emotions, so he just squeezed her fingers, grateful that his healing had come in leaps and bounds and in directions that he'd had no inkling were even possible. Wait until he told Zander.

Epilogue

YVONNE BRITMAN STOOD outside the front doors of Hathaway House. Lord, this was not how she wanted to return. When she'd left, she had been in tears, a broken woman in so many ways and yet one put back together in so many other ways. She'd been so determined to be someone—someone new. Someone who could handle the changes in her life, prepped to be a success regardless of physical injuries. She'd been so sure she could rise to the top …

As she stood here for a long moment staring at the entrance, a woman opened up the door and asked, "Are you coming inside? Would you like some help?"

Yvonne smiled and nodded, and, using her arm crutches, made her way slowly up the ramp.

"Most of the time," the woman noted, "people come by ambulance."

"I was really hoping not to," Yvonne replied.

At the sound of her voice, the other woman gasped. "Oh my. Yvonne?"

Dani. Yvonne let Dani's arms wrap around her in the gentlest of hugs, bringing tears to her eyes. "As much as I love you guys to bits, I really, really, *really* didn't want to come back here."

"Not like this, I'm sure," Dani noted. "However, anytime we can help a former graduate of this place, we're here for them. When you called back about the IT interview, your request to return as a patient was not what I expected."

"Well, a car accident was not what I expected to happen either."

"Nor having it happen on a crosswalk either," Dani added. "You certainly didn't have to drive yourself here today."

"Yet it was hard for me *not* to," she replied. "I … I left this place. I left it in good conscience. I left it thinking that I was done with rehab forever. And yet here I am."

"I'm not sure if anybody's injuries are ever healed forever," Dani clarified. "So don't put that kind of pressure on yourself," she whispered.

As Yvonne made her way into the front lobby, she collapsed onto the nearest chair, the shudders racking through her body.

"And, of course, you did too much already," Dani scolded her.

"No, just a show of pride. Stiff, ugly, cold-at-night pride."

Dani winced. "I haven't told him, you know?"

She nodded. "That's probably for the best. He'll see me when he sees me, and we'll deal with it then."

"Are you sure?" Dani asked. "If it were me, I would want a little bit of notice."

"Nope, maybe we'll hash it out this time around."

"I hope so," Dani said. "He's a good man."

"He's the best, but that didn't mean it was right to leave at the time."

"That's for you guys to figure out," Dani suggested. "In the meantime, I'm so sorry for what happened to bring you back to us, but you're here now, and we'll help. We will take care of you."

Yvonne looked up at her old friend and nodded slowly. "And you have no idea how grateful I am for the opportunity to come back."

"Even with Dennis here?" Dani teased.

"Maybe especially because Dennis is here," she admitted, with a nod. "It's time. Whether that guy knows it or not, it's time."

"Good luck with that. Dennis is many things, but he cares for everybody else first. His needs come dead last."

"Well, this time," Yvonne declared, "he just might have to deal with his own feelings because I'm not going away. Not again."

This concludes Book 24 of Hathaway House: Xavier.
Read about Yvonne: Hathaway House, Book 25

Hathaway House: Yvonne
(Book #25)

Welcome to Hathaway House. Rehab Center. Safe Haven. Second chance at life and love.

Yvonne made a mistake leaving Hathaway House and walking away from Dennis. Hugely comforting and caring man that he was, she had been so determined to move forward and to be someone independent that she couldn't see what he had to offer. Until it was too late.

Dennis could only love and let her go years ago. Now she's returned to Hathaway House—injured again, broken inside, emotionally devastated, and worn out from the hard fight she has endured over the last five years. And Dennis is forced to the sidelines, watching as the woman he loves once again struggles to work toward her new more-broken reality.

If only she see could see this as a second chance for both of them …

Find Book 25 here!
To find out more visit Dale Mayer's website.
https://geni.us/DMSYvonne

Author's Note

Thank you for reading Xavier: Hathaway House, Book 24! If you enjoyed the book, please take a moment and leave a short review.

Dear reader,

I love to hear from readers, and you can contact me at my website: www.dalemayer.com or at my Facebook author page. To be informed of new releases and special offers, sign up for my newsletter or follow me on BookBub. And if you are interested in joining Dale Mayer's Reader Group, here is the Facebook sign up page.
http://geni.us/DaleMayerFBGroup

Cheers,
Dale Mayer

About the Author

Dale Mayer is a *USA Today* best-selling author, best known for her SEALs military romances, her Psychic Visions series, and her Lovely Lethal Garden cozy series. Her contemporary romances are raw and full of passion and emotion (Broken But … Mending, Hathaway House series). Her thrillers will keep you guessing (Kate Morgan, By Death series), and her romantic comedies will keep you giggling (*It's a Dog's Life*, a stand-alone novella; and the Broken Protocols series, starring Charming Marvin, the cat).

Dale honors the stories that come to her—and some of them are crazy, break all the rules and cross multiple genres!

To go with her fiction, she also writes nonfiction in many different fields, with books available on résumé writing, companion gardening, and the US mortgage system. All her books are available in print and ebook format.

Connect with Dale Mayer Online

Dale's Website – www.dalemayer.com
Twitter – @DaleMayer
Facebook Page – geni.us/DaleMayerFBFanPage
Facebook Group – geni.us/DaleMayerFBGroup
BookBub – geni.us/DaleMayerBookbub
Instagram – geni.us/DaleMayerInstagram
Goodreads – geni.us/DaleMayerGoodreads
Newsletter – geni.us/DaleNews

www.ingramcontent.com/pod-product-compliance
Lightning Source LLC
Chambersburg PA
CBHW070353200726
48294CB00003B/884